And Then You Fall

DEDICATION

This book is dedicated to all the insecure writers out there. This is the dumbest job and it never gets easier, but every now and then when a reader tells you they enjoyed your book, it makes it all worth it.

Acknowledgments

Chris – Thank you for always supporting me.

DJ – Dude.

Suzanne S. – Thank you for being my very best yet evil editor.

Katie S. – Thank you for helping me make the story better.

TO:

Jennifer Lynn

Carol Anne S.

Amy L.

Julie D.

Sam S.

Nick M.

Tara T.

Nick P.

Jason B.

Thank you guys for answering all of my questions, or helping me read, or edit, or stay partially sane. Any errors are my own.

And Then You Fall

A Maguire's Corner Novel

Heather M. Gardner

CHAPTER ONE

"Where the hell are all my units?"

Bobby Maguire had been working with Police Chief Jack Munro for a while, but just about anyone would recognize the tension in his boss's voice over the radio. The Maguire's Corner Police Department had a small window to make this drug bust and stop the dealer's operation before they closed up shop and relocated. They were all feeling the pressure.

"Rear Unit in position."

Officer Nick Ward responded first. Three other officers rounded out Nick's team and they held position around the back of a dilapidated farmhouse, watching the doors and windows for activity. At this point, the worst thing that could go wrong would be getting caught by the dealers while they were still setting up their raid.

"K-9 Unit in position."

His voice quiet and calm, Officer Sean Rafferty replied through the earpiece. The new guy, along with his German Shepard Mick, had proven to be an important addition to the MCPD. The dog's initial sweep of the lockers at the high school had uncovered small baggies full of heroin, leading them to their 'not-completely-trustworthy' source, and this raid.

"AC Maguire?"

Jack's voice resonated through his earpiece in a short heated burst that could scorch the ears of the most seasoned cop. Bobby knew the chief had serious reservations conducting this evening raid, a plan that had the potential to go wrong at any moment, which meant Jack might call an audible and pack the whole thing up.

"Rifleman in position, Chief."

Hidden in a clump of maples, Bobby stood with the barrel of his gun resting on a low branch. Most of the leaves had already fallen off this tree and he had an unobstructed view of all but one side of the house. He tilted his head right and left, cracking his neck. He checked his rifle again. Through his scope he could see Rafferty and Mick crouched down in the tall grass toward the front corner of the structure.

"Officer Douglas, please report."

"Front Unit is in position, Chief. Thermal camera shows five suspects standing inside the main room. There's a sixth suspect alone in a room on the north side of the building."

"What's he doing?" Jack asked.

"He appears to be taking a crap."

"Thank you. Everyone hold."

Now, they'd just have to wait and see. Jack could go either way at this point. It wasn't that the chief thought the team couldn't handle this kind of operation. They'd been trained on conducting raids, response tactics, close quarters combat, and contingency plans. But, Jack wouldn't relax until all the bad guys were in cuffs and all the good guys were headed home.

"We go in five...."

Bobby's adrenaline spiked and he took slow breaths to control the surge. His sharpshooting skills put him further from the action than he liked. He missed charging through the front door with the team. Still, he could feel the intensity in the chilled air. The anticipation.

"Four...."

His grip tightened on his rifle. Staring through the scope he made calculation adjustments in his head. Wind, distance, temperature. The position of his team. The location of the drug dealers.

"Three...."

His gut clenched. Breathe. Focus. Observe. Take out any stragglers.

"Two...."

Safety off.

"Go."

Listening to the chatter through his headset, Bobby could picture the entire engagement in his mind. Battering ram to the front door. Five officers enter, fanning out. Shouts of *Police get down.* Suspects pushed to the floor and secured. More shouting as the suspect from the bathroom runs for the back door, only to be met by more officers. Multiple calls of *Clear* as the house is searched room by room.

Bobby scanned the perimeter of the building again. Then again. No movement. No suspects. No problem. Safety on. He removed the magazine and cleared his rifle. At this rate he might still catch the last quarter of the football game by the time they packed up and got out of here.

"Gun!"

Swinging around, Bobby shoved the barrel of his weapon back onto the branch. Checking the scope, he slammed the magazine home, racking the first round. Where the hell did a seventh person come from? Shots rang out, incredibly loud in his ears, yet he couldn't see anyone.

"I'm hit!"

"He's running."

The eyepiece dug into Bobby's skin as he tucked the piece of hardware in closer. There. Appearing from the far side of the house.

"AC Maguire. Do you have him?"

Safety off.

He followed the movement of the suspect as he took off, away from Bobby on foot. He slowed his breathing, timing the steps of the man, leading him, calculating the distance, changing the angle. Breathe in, finger on the trigger, breathe out, pull the trigger.

The bullet's impact jerked the suspect sideways and he fell to the ground. Bobby could hear his surprised shout from 150 yards away. Twice the man tried to get back up, to continue his run for freedom, but his injured leg wouldn't cooperate. The K-9 stood growling over him before he could make a third attempt.

"Suspect in custody."

Bobby continued to survey the area for a long time before he finally secured his weapon again. He ran his palms back and forth over his short dark hair. Dammit. How had they all missed him? Blowing out a huge breath, he jogged toward the scene, muttering to himself. Where had that seventh person come from?

The ambulance they'd kept on stand-by had already pulled up to the house and Bobby stopped at the back. Nick sat on the end of the stretcher, blood soaking into his uniform shirt sleeve from his upper arm. A very pretty EMT, with long black hair and a pair of giant scissors, cut away his sleeve.

"This guy gonna live, Min?"

"Hey, Bobby. He should be fine with a good scrub and a couple of stitches."

"Glad to hear that. You okay, Nick?"

"Yeah. Stings like a bitc – sorry, Min. I'll be fine. I have no idea where that guy came from."

"You and me both. We'll figure it out. I'm just glad he shoots worse than you do."

"You got him, right?"

"Of course, and just for you, he'll never walk without a limp. Go home after the hospital, Nick. You can write up your report tomorrow."

"Thanks, ACM."

Bobby shook his head at the new abbreviation as he walked away. His fellow officers were still trying out variations of his name and rank since his promotion to Assistant Chief. Jack had settled on AC Maguire, but the guys didn't like it. Bobby considered himself lucky they weren't calling him Ass. Chief anymore.

After stowing his equipment in one of the police cars now on scene, Bobby walked to where Jack stood over the man writhing on the ground, holding his knee. His moans were whiney and Bobby toyed with the idea of knocking him unconscious while they waited for the second ambulance. Staring harder at the man, willing him to shut up, recognition dawned on him.

"Shit."

Jack's frosty gaze snapped to him. He moved a few feet away, motioning Bobby to follow.

"Did you just make a positive ID of our shooter?"

Bobby blew out a breath. "Second-in-command at the Unite Today compound and Drake's heir-apparent, August Drake."

This time Jack cursed. Bobby understood his boss's pain. Nothing good would come from this. The Unite Today group, which the locals referred to as 'The Cult', normally kept things low key. Everyone knew they were up to stuff, just not what that stuff might be, or if it was in fact illegal. Recently their actions had touched the town in a negative way. One of their members currently sat in the county jail on arson and attempted murder charges.

Bobby rubbed the back of his neck. "Well, now we have our connection between the drugs and Unite Today."

"Do you think Drake is even aware of his kid's drug operation?"

"I can't imagine August being the brains behind this. He barely graduated high school and he doesn't exactly have Drake's – entrepreneurial skills."

"True." Jack shook his head. "This is going to get complicated."

"You think when we book his son on drug charges, and attempted murder of a police officer, Drake might take that as a personal insult?"

"Yes. Yes, I do."

"Yeah, so do I."

The second ambulance approached them and the chief ordered the suspect to be cuffed and escorted at all times. Then Jack read him his rights, personally, while another officer filmed the whole thing. Jack had switched to CYA mode. Cover Your Ass.

The police and Unite Today had steered clear of each other for years. But, with the arsons this past summer, and now this drug problem becoming more prevalent in Maguire's Corner, that time had passed. The members of Unite Today were now in MCPD's direct line of sight.

"AC Maguire, let's wrap this up and clear the scene. I want everything on record as soon as possible and completely by the book. Film as much as we can. No shortcuts, no mistakes."

"Got it, Chief. I'll head over to the house to check on their progress."

"Hey!" August let out a shout as Bobby turned away. "Maguire! Did you pull the trigger?"

Bobby sized up the man handcuffed to the stretcher, considering if he should bother to respond, but decided against it. There wouldn't be anything he could say that August wouldn't try to twist.

"Maguire! You know what Drake's gonna do when he finds out you shot me?"

Bobby kept walking. He had so many great comebacks to that question yet he refused to give the guy more verbal ammunition. Heading to the house, he could still hear August bellowing while they packed him in the ambulance.

CHAPTER TWO

Cassidy hadn't stopped moving since breakfast, which had been hastily eaten over the sink before the sun had come up. She still had plenty to check off her to-do list for tonight's grand opening of the Brewhouse and her first public beer tasting. After all the hard work and sacrifice, everything started to come together, and that nervous feeling plaguing her, rolled into excitement.

She'd taken a huge leap of faith and partnered with her friends, the O'Hart twins, to convert an old barn, off County Route One, into a fully functioning brewery/bar/restaurant. They'd accomplished so much in six months and they had a lot to be proud of.

Taylor and Tyler had literally done most of the heavy lifting and created a homey, rustic atmosphere for the patrons, a state-of-the-art brewing room for her, and a world class kitchen for their newly hired chef. She'd brewed a few thousand gallons of her own signature beers into kegs and bottles as her contribution. It would all be worth it when the doors finally opened to eager customers.

Cassidy needed to get her butt moving and get some work done before any of those customers would be allowed in at 6:00 pm. There were more stools to assemble and then she could move on to washing mugs and pint glasses. She had a few more things to hang and then give the bar top one last shine.

The bar's cordless phone buzzed in her back pocket. She checked the screen and pushed the answer button, wedged the phone between her ear and her shoulder and tightened another screw on the stool.

"Maguire's Mugs Brewhouse, this is Cassidy."

"It's Taylor. Didn't you know it was me?"

The three of them had been working so closely for months they were practically living in each other's pockets and on the verge of driving each other nuts.

"Yes, I can read the caller ID. I'm just trying different phone greetings. What's up?"

"Tyler's got me picking up lunch on my way back from the hardware store. You want?"

"It's barely past breakfast and you're already making plans for lunch?"

"It's not me. It's Tyler. You know he's always thinking about his next meal."

"Of course. What did you guys choose today?"

"Pizza."

She flipped the completed stool over and set it on the floor. "Again?"

"We're creatures of habit."

"Creatures sounds about right." The twins made it their mission to gross her out whenever possible. That included weird foods, showing her every injury they acquired each day, and the worst, sharing every single nasty smell they could create with their bodies. "I'm in. Make sure mine doesn't have any of that pepperoni on it."

"You said extra roni?"

"Extra cheese."

"Fine. So, we gonna be ready on time? You need any help in there?"

She looked around the room, pleased with the way it was shaping up. It no longer resembled a run down, abandoned barn. It had warmth and character oozing from every scrubbed corner. "I'm good. I've got to go out for a bit and then I'm back to finish up for the tasting extravaganza!"

"How's the social media looking?"

"Really great. All our curious neighbors are clamoring to get here first."

"That's what I like to hear. The chef and his staff are getting acquainted with the kitchen?"

"Yep. Lots of pot and pan noises coming from back there, so I'm hoping there's also cooking going on. What are you getting at the hardware store?"

"I've got to pick up more light bulbs, some washers, and a door knob. You need to add to my list?"

"Um...some picture hanger thingies."

"Is that a technical term?"

She smiled. "It is. It'll say 'thingies' right on the box."

"Okay. I'll see you in a couple hours."

Cassidy worked hard to finish off at least half her list and then cleaned up her mess. She had more to do, but first, she had an errand to run that she'd kept putting off and she no longer had any excuse to ignore it. She texted the twins to tell them she'd be back in an hour, then jumped in her car and drove into town.

SUNDAY MORNINGS IN Bobby's world were the best, designed for sleeping in, swimming laps, followed by outrageously delicious pancakes at his aunt's restaurant. Bobby currently held the record for eating the most pancakes at one sitting, ten for those keeping track, but normally he had a regular order with eggs, and extra bacon on the side. As far as Bobby was concerned, there were no greater words in the English language than 'extra bacon'.

Rolling over in his king size bed, he checked the clock. 6:00 am. Perfect. He threw on his swim trunks, sweatshirt, and flip-flops, grabbed a towel and his keys and headed to the door. His apartment complex happened to be situated next to the local community center and for a small fee the tenants had complete access to the indoor heated pool and other facilities.

A hold-over from his high school swim team days, Bobby loved to swim and he made use of every opportunity to get in the water. He could swim laps for hours and not get tired of it. He'd tried other cardio exercise, but none of them gave him the same 'runner's high' that he got in the pool.

On this early fall morning, the complex stood empty and the smooth water beckoned. Muscle memory took over his freestyle strokes and his mind wandered. In the time it took him to complete his routine, he'd figured out the only place August Drake could have stood during the raid to avoid the thermal imaging camera.

August must have been on the other side of the sliding glass doors located on the far side of the building. Only the glass would've been able to block him from the camera. Had it been good timing that he'd stood in the only place the camera couldn't read him or had he been forewarned of their arrival? Another piece of the puzzle to discuss with Jack.

Bobby climbed out of the pool just as the lifeguard showed up. Looking forward to digging into those well-deserved pancakes, he headed back to his place. As he reached his doorway he stopped short at the sight of a small basket on his welcome mat.

The odds of that basket containing muffins? With his luck lately? Zilch. The longer he stared at it, the more he thought it might be a baby's bassinet with a hood and some blue ribbons. Bobby's gut churned. His head filled with questions. Did the basket have a baby in it? Did he get someone pregnant? Would this be his kid, abandoned on his doorstep? He kneeled down to check under the blanket.

Tugging back the cotton, it became clear that a doll had been wrapped up in the blue blanket. Painfully, the air pushed out of his lungs. Not a real baby. His temporary relief at being spared child support payments dissipated when he noticed the red liquid staining the doll's clothing. His head dropped, shoulders slumping. He knew who'd left it. This had to be another 'gift' from his friendly neighborhood stalker, Theresa.

Bobby stood to unlock his door, then used his towel to pick up the basket and bring it inside. He put on a pair of gloves from the police bag he'd grabbed from his garage and using the camera on his phone, he methodically took pictures as he removed everything from inside the basket. The queasy feeling in his stomach returned as he checked through all of it until he found the note he knew she would leave for him.

This could have been our baby, but you killed any possibility of that when you left me. You never gave us a chance. I hate you.

Heartwarming and psychotic. Great. He'd only had a couple of dates with Theresa in the spring before he'd ended things with her. She'd gotten way too attached, way too quickly. She didn't take the end of their short association well and the fallout kept coming.

Bobby put the basket, and its contents, into a black plastic bag, carried it out to his car, and put it in the trunk with all the other 'Crazy Waitress Theresa' memorabilia she'd left him, like the dead flowers and ripped photographs. She should be running out of steam, but this unwanted gift might be the worst thing she'd done so far.

The cost to fix the paint job after she scratched the hell out of his 1969 Ford Mustang Boss 429 still pained him. Okay, that would be the worst thing she'd done. It hurt worse than when she sliced his arm with a broken wine glass and he had to get stitches.

He'd thought if he ignored her behavior she'd get bored and move on, but it seemed to actually escalate her mania instead. It might be past time to talk to Jack about her and Bobby knew because he'd waited this long to tell him, his boss would be pissed.

CHAPTER THREE

Cassidy parked in the visitor's lot of a small apartment complex and searched for a sign to tell her where apartment 13 would be. Wandering the sidewalks, and admiring the well-kept gardens in their autumn colors, she finally found the right door. Checking her watch, she realized the early hour. Maybe she should wait. Not everyone liked to rise and shine as early as she did.

She quickly knocked before she could change her mind. No one answered. It would totally suck if she had to come back. She lifted her fist to knock again and the door swung wide.

"Egads!"

Not only did the whoosh of the door being yanked open surprise her, but the sight of Bobby Maguire standing on his threshold in nothing but low-riding swim trunks nearly made her swoon. She clamped her lips shut so she wouldn't say anything else out loud while ogling his smooth lean-muscled chest and his kick-ass abs.

His gaze took her in head to toe. "Pardon?"

"I'm aware that's how this whole 'knock-and-answer-the-door-thing' works, but you startled me."

His eyebrows drew together making a cute little 'v' over his nose. "Can I help you?"

"Well, I came here to make you a proposition..." She spotted something in his grip. "But, I don't think you need to be armed to hear it."

The hand containing a black firearm moved further behind his leg. "I'm about to close this door unless you tell me what you want."

She should go. Her instincts were usually spot-on. He clearly didn't want company. On the other hand, she knew she wouldn't get a chance to return anytime soon. She gathered her courage to declare her intentions before she chickened out.

"Would you be interested in a little work under the table?"

He shook his head. "You know I'm a cop, right?"

"Art work. I mean your art work. You used to draw and sketch stuff."

Bobby's eyes widened, then narrowed. "How do you know that?"

"How do I...huh?" He had to be kidding with her, right?

"Ma'am, I'm not sure what your game is here, but I need to get moving." He started to close the door.

"Ma'am?" He's not kidding. "Wait. Okay. My name's Cassidy. I was like a year behind you all through high school."

She pushed her sunglasses up on top of her head to reveal her best feature, her bright silvery-grey eyes. They'd been called everything from pretty to surreal to creepy. He stared at her for a long moment. His face didn't register recognition.

Sure, she didn't look exactly the same, but she'd like to think she'd kept her youthful appearance even several years out of school. There were a few minor changes. Her thick black hair now reached the middle of her back and had deep purple streaks running through it. Her face had slimmed out, but she still had great curves in all the right places. Her clothing choices probably remained the most unchanged, predominately black, denim and leather.

"I'm sorry. I don't remember you from school."

A wave of annoyance flushed her skin. Bobby's reputation with knowing every woman in town must be all hype. She hadn't expected to have to remind him that he knew her.

"Well, that just figures. So, I'm the Brewmaster at Maguire's Mugs Brewhouse."

"The O'Hart's place?"

She grabbed the ends of her own hair and pulled down hard. If she had a nickel for every time someone called it that. "Yes. We're calling it the Brewhouse for short. Tyler, Taylor, and I. We're all partners." She crossed her arms over her chest. "Do you want to hear about my offer or not?"

"Sure." He took a step closer to her, his chest inches from her nose, smelling like chlorine and well-developed man. He looked in all directions before he stepped back into his house. "Come on in."

Walking in behind him, she witnessed him placing his gun into a safe installed in the wall. He closed the small door with a snap. Did he always answer the door armed and if so, why? She knew his family had gone through some trouble in the last year, but she didn't think it warranted that kind of paranoia.

Intrigued to know more about the man beside her, she did a quick survey of his living room. Nice furniture. Lots of oak. Framed photos on the mantle. Big screen TV on the entertainment center. Game console. Clean. Too clean for a guy. And the air conditioner had to be on because it felt like winter had come to town - inside.

"You drink coffee, Cassidy?"

She hid her frown when he put a T-shirt on over all that tanned skin. "Not exclusively."

His wide grin caused all her girly parts to sigh. She hadn't known she would be so attracted to this grown-up version of Bobby Maguire. She knew better than to ignore her gut reactions, now she embraced them.

"How about now? Would you like some coffee?"

"I'd love some."

BOBBY LED HER TO HIS kitchen, offering her a seat at the table. He'd expected the worst when he'd opened the front door. Another 'present' from Theresa or an unwelcome visit from one of Drake's henchmen. What a surprise to find such a stunning woman on his welcome mat.

He moved to the cabinet to grab clean coffee mugs. For a moment he thought she might be a Unite Today member, but the way she talked changed his mind. Really, she'd had him at 'proposition' and 'under the table'. Something about her had him terribly curious. And those eyes. When her sunglasses came off, his heart skipped a few beats.

Cassidy spun the salt shaker on the scarred oak table. "So, I suppose I should first ask if you still sketch?"

"Sometimes."

"Good, cause here's the thing. I want a certain look for the beer bottle labels. In my opinion, the labels need to be created specifically for each flavor of beer, not just one general design for our brand. Do you remember that black and white drawing you did of the creek in Maguire's Corner Park? The one with the willow tree limbs dragging in the water? You entered it in the art show."

His eyebrows shot straight up. "I drew that, what, seven or eight years ago? You remember it?"

"Mmm hmm. I loved it and I want that sketch-look on all the labels."

"You're serious?" Bobby poured coffee into the mugs. "You want me to do the art for the bar?"

The shaker slipped from her fingers, spilling some of its contents on the table. "Brewhouse." Cassidy stood, brushed the grains into her cupped hand, tossed a little over her shoulder, dumped the rest into his sink, and then put the shaker back with its partner when she sat back down. "If you still do that kind of stuff, yeah."

He held back a snort of laughter. Who does that? Most people would have just brushed the spilled salt onto the floor. "If you're trying to prevent bad luck, you should throw that over your left shoulder." He put a steaming mug in front of her. "Do you put anything in your coffee?"

She blinked up at him. "Blood of a virgin and the eye of a newt."

"How about cream and sugar?"

"That works, too."

He could be imagining that the room seemed brighter with her in it. And more musical with all those dangly earrings she wore. Where the hell had she been hiding? Funny. Sarcastic. Beautiful, yes, but more like exotic or remarkable. Especially those eyes. It's like they had an inner glow.

He set the sugar, creamer, and spoons in the center of the table. Before he sat down he reached into a kitchen drawer and pulled out paper and a pencil. "Tell me more about your proposition."

"We're starting off with our four strongest beer recipes. We'll add more eventually and change them seasonally. The first priority is to replace the current generic look with your art. You still with me?"

"I think so."

She pulled a piece of paper from her pocket and unfolded it. "I've been jotting down ideas. When I have them. About each beer." She took a sip of her coffee. "Mmmm. Oh, God, that's good." She took a bigger gulp. "Yes. Hot damn! You should come tonight."

"What's that now?" She had him half-hard just complimenting his coffee and he wasn't sure where that sentence might be headed.

"To the beer tasting."

"Right. Your grand opening." Bobby had been on the fence about going, however, her very presence in his kitchen sealed the deal.

"Yes! I kinda waited forever to get over here and ask you, but tonight would be the perfect opportunity for you to taste all the beers and maybe you'll get your own ideas."

"Maybe I will." He read through her suggestions, ignoring the sizzle of want coursing through him. It wouldn't do him any good to get mixed up with someone he needed to work closely with. "These should help. You've put some real thought into them. I'll need to take some photos of these landmarks before I start drawing. Then maybe a week or so to sketch. Does that work for you?"

"Absolutely." Cassidy downed her coffee like a college kid chugged beer at a frat party. "Wooh. My second favorite beverage. After we get the labels done, I'd like to have a mural painted in the bar."

"Shouldn't you wait to see what I come up with first?"

"Already know what I like or I wouldn't be here."

He folded her paper back up. "What if I haven't drawn a damn thing since college?"

She raised her eyebrows. "Is that true?"

"No."

She stood, her olive-drab jacket opening enough to reveal her Harley shirt had been tied in a knot at her waist showing a patch of creamy skin over her black denim jeans. Earlier, when she'd grown frustrated with him, a light blush had bloomed across her neck. He wondered how far down that rose color went. He'd bet good money she blushed right before she...

"Let's be real. Draw for me. If I don't like them, I'll tell you the absolute truth. If I do like them, I'll pay you per label you create for the Brewhouse. The mural will be a separate job. Does this meet with your approval?"

He put out his hand and she grasped it hard. "You've got a deal, Cassidy."

"All right, then, Bobby. If you come tonight, come thirsty."

CHAPTER FOUR

"This area is for employees only, Miss. I'm gonna have to ask you to head back out to the front of the establishment."

Had Tyler and Taylor only listened to her, there would be ropes up across the hall tonight, so Cassidy wouldn't have to show yet another nosey customer how to get back to the bar.

"I'm looking for your bathrooms."

"You passed them on the way here." Note to self, put more lights around the bathroom area.

"Sorry. I was texting and missed it."

Maybe some arrows on the floor, too. "No problem." Cassidy didn't see a phone in the woman's hand, but she supposed she could have put it away already. She shifted the boxes in her arms. "Let me walk you back."

"That would be great. You must be Cassidy."

"That's correct."

"I'm Theresa. So, what do you do here?"

Cassidy reined in her snappy comeback. She had to be nice to the customers, even if they wore their skirt real short and their blonde hair so teased a squirrel could take up residence in there and no one would know. "I make the beer."

"I thought Taylor and Tyler did that?"

"Nope. All me. They did all the work on the building."

"And just in time too, this place was ready to fall down to the ground. How in the world did you manage to get so many important people to show up to your little party?"

Cassidy remembered being intimidated by girls like this one back in high school. "It may have something to do with the free beer." Not so much anymore.

"The Mayor is here. Judge Allan. Assistant Chief Maguire."

Assistant Chief Maguire. That sounded so formal and important. Cassidy still had trouble picturing Bobby as anything but a swim jock, charming all the pretty girls wherever he went.

Cassidy stopped in the hall. "I'm glad Bobby could make it."

The woman moved a little closer, like she was sharing a secret. "He's my boyfriend." She had a big smile on her face when she moved back.

Boyfriend? Cassidy had never heard that word used in the same sentence with Bobby's name before. Why would hearing it now fill her with disappointment?

"Okay. Great, well, it was nice of y'all to come tonight. Here is the women's restroom. I hope you come back again."

"Sure. Maybe I'll see you around."

Cassidy didn't like to instantly judge people, but something about Theresa gave her the heebie jeebies. She headed back to the bar, pleased to see a large crowd remained after the initial free tasting. They were staying to drink her beer, which meant something had finally gone right in her life, and that felt amazing. As long as people enjoyed it, she'd keep making it.

She set down the boxes she'd grabbed from the storeroom. Bobby Maguire sat at the end of the handcrafted bar top, still hot fully dressed. Out of all the men she might fancy, it had to be Bobby? The player, the heartbreaker, the one to stay away from? Yet, she wanted to fall into those suede brown eyes and stay awhile. Her choice had been made for her though. Apparently, he had a girlfriend.

Cassidy worked her way down the bar, taking drink orders, removing empty mugs, and making change. When she reached him she gave him a smile. "Hey."

"Hey. What am I drinking? Tyler handed it to me."

'Um...looks like he gave you the unfiltered wheat beer. Do you like it?"

"It may be my new favorite beer."

Another customer ordered and she filled his mug at the tap. "Then I've done my German ancestors proud. It's one of the first brews I made."

"Well, now I like you even more."

"Careful. Don't say that too loud." She grabbed a bar rag and wiped down the wood. "I just met your girlfriend by the bathroom."

Bobby snorted. "Not likely. I'm not dating anyone."

"Except your girlfriend."

"Except I don't have a girlfriend."

"That would be news to her, I'm sure." Cassidy tossed the dirty towel into the pail marked linens, then leaned on the bar. "She said her name was Theresa."

Bobby's smile disappeared and his eyes narrowed. He turned on his stool and searched the room, scanning the people in it like a robot might.

"Do you see her now, Cassidy?"

"No, I don't."

His shoulders relaxed. He turned back to the bar and picked up his beer. "Theresa is not, nor has she ever been, my girlfriend."

"Good. I don't mean good like ... you know what? Never mind." She picked up a clean bar rag and threw it over her shoulder.

Bobby tapped a finger on the bar top. "You got a little flustered there."

"No, I didn't." She'd never admit it out loud, yet she feared her heated cheeks might be giving her away. "So, do you want to try a dark beer or a lager next?"

He made his eyebrows waggle. "I'd like to sample everything you have available."

She laughed as she clapped her hands together, rubbing them against each other. "Everything? An adventurous man. I like that."

Bobby emptied his drink and slid it toward Cassidy. "I'll be back tomorrow to take some pictures during the day. Will you be here?"

"I'm always here. I live in the loft. It's a real short commute to work."

"You still have family in town?"

She placed his mug with the other dirty ones. "Just me now." A pang of loss broke over her, but faded. Each day got slightly easier. "Lost my mom recently."

"I'm sorry to hear that. What was her name?"

"Ruby."

"Was she a nice lady? A good mom?"

"Yeah, she was the best."

"What about your dad?"

Her dad? A wave of anger threatened to surface, but she shook it off. She refused to let thoughts of him ruin her night. "So many questions. You studyin' for the detective's exam or something?"

"Sorry." Bobby held his hands up in mock surrender. "I think my boss may be rubbing off on me."

She poured a pint and set it in front of him. "This is our copper lager. It will be crisp with a hint of honey."

"This looks great, but I'm gonna need some food to go with it. I missed, well, all my meals today."

"You want a menu?"

He held her gaze for a moment. "Surprise me."

Stepping over to the register she tapped on the screen. "It should only be a few minutes. If you'll pardon me a moment, I see Taylor and I need to tell him something."

BOBBY MADE NO EXCUSES watching her walk away in her black jeans and purple combat boots. That girl intrigued the hell out of him. He should talk to his sister about her. Maggie remembered everyone and everything from school and beyond. He barely recalled what classes he'd taken since he hadn't spent a lot of time in them.

He sipped his beer. Damn, that tasted delicious. She had a real gift. He spotted Cassidy to his right talking to O'Hart and each time Taylor said something she would laugh and then he casually draped his arm around her shoulders. Was that a friendly gesture? They looked more than friendly. Were they together? Why did that make him feel, unsettled?

She ducked under Taylor's arm, disappearing down a hallway Bobby assumed led to the kitchen. He shouldn't care one way or the other since he basically only met her today. The adult her, anyway. So, it shouldn't bother him that they looked very comfortable with each other. Right?

He checked the whole room again. No sign of Theresa. He should have talked to Jack about her, but he'd completely chickened out. Not a proud moment in his life. He just didn't want to disappoint his best friend and boss.

Cassidy returned, placing a plate in front of him with a giant hamburger and a pile of golden fries.

"That was fast."

"This is on me."

"Thank you, but you don't have to do that."

"You're helping me out. It's the least I can do."

"I appreciate that." He lifted the top bun. He should ask her to marry him right now. The burger was smothered in cheese and bacon. "Good thing I don't have any cardiac issues."

She gave him a slow smile. "Yet."

"Very funny. There are easier ways to kill me."

"You finished your beer. What do you want to try next?"

"You seem to be anticipating my needs, you choose."

Bobby's first bite had him silently thanking the universe for beef and bacon. He used his napkin to catch the juice before it ran down his chin.

"Good, right? Everything is local. The meat, the cheese, even the bread. This is our amber ale." She set a new glass in front of him. "Should go great with your meal."

"What are you doing for the rest of my life?"

Her smile held him transfixed, like a siren luring him in. "Baby, I don't think you can handle all this."

She never should have said that. That most certainly sounded like a dare to him. So much for not mixing business with pleasure. "You may be right, but you can't blame a man for trying."

CHAPTER FIVE

"Remember your stance. Lean in. Keep your weight forward. Bend your knees, slightly. Take the shot."

Bobby stood next to his cousin, Emily, while she prepared to fire her new handgun in the shooting range located in the basement of the police station. She'd been 'preparing' for more than ten minutes.

"Take the shot."

Emily blew the bangs off her forehead. "Quiet, Bobby."

Good. She could hear him shouting over their ear protection. "He's not going to wait for you to get comfortable. Take the shot."

His comment was a low blow and he knew it. She would be well aware that when Bobby said 'he' he meant Artie Blake, Jr., a complete psychopath, that had attacked Emily and police officer Avery Bailey in front of the station back in January. She'd sustained injuries that nearly killed her and Avery had died protecting her.

She lowered her head, took a deep breath, and proceeded to start her preparations all over again. At this rate she'd never fire the damn weapon. How could he make her understand that she didn't have all the time in the world?

"You may not be so lucky next time. It's you or him, Emily. It's me or him. It's anyone or him. Take the shot."

"Lucky? You call what I went through lucky?"

"You know what I mean."

Dammit. All she had to do was pull the trigger. Just pull it. Emily set her feet again. He groaned and before she could start arranging herself all over again, Bobby pulled his duty weapon and rapidly emptied the magazine into the silhouette at the end of the lane next to hers.

"You're dead, Emily." Bobby released the empty magazine, ramming in a full one, then used the release button to send the slide home.

"You didn't even give me a chance."

"Neither would he. Ready, aim, fire. That's what you need to do. Ready your body and mind. Aim for the target. Fire the weapon."

"I'm trying."

"No, you're preparing. Take the shot."

Emily took another deep breath, squared her shoulders and leaned forward. Raising her gun she took aim at her own silhouette.

"Don't think. Take the shot. He's coming. He's going to kill you. Shoot him."

When she started to shake, he clamped his hands over hers, lowering and removing her weapon carefully from her grip. He unloaded her gun, setting the parts on the high counter next to them.

Bobby pulled the cord holding in his ear plugs. "You're not ready. Come back in a month."

"A month?" Emily shook out her hands and then wiped them on her pants. "That's too long. I know I can do it. I just can't seem to get through all the steps yet."

"No, you can't pull the trigger. Once you do, everything else will fall into place."

"I want to."

Bobby regarded her for a moment, before he shrugged. "You may never be that kind of person, Emily, and that's fine. Don't tie yourself up about it."

"You mean be like you?"

He frowned down at her. "What's that supposed to mean?"

"The kind of person who turns everything off to get through his day."

"Don't be so dramatic."

"You could just tell me what's going on with you, Bobby. That way Maggie, Kate, and I wouldn't have to dig so hard."

And they had been digging. For weeks. Problem #450 living in a small town with most of your family; there's no escaping them. "Nothing's going on. I'm good."

"You don't seem good. You seem ... angry."

"Well, I'm not. What I am is on duty in about twenty minutes. Why don't you show yourself out and I'll deal with this." He waved his hand over the hardware.

Emily grinned. "Did you just dismiss me?"

"You know if you don't like the way I do things you can ask Jack to teach you how to shoot."

"See?" She pointed at him. "That! That's not normal. The real Bobby would tell me he's better at this than Jack is, or ever could be, and he would never let anyone else teach me. Who are you and what have you done with my cousin?"

"You're as bad as Maggie and Kate. Stop nagging me." Bobby scrubbed his hand over his face, reigning in his anger. He knew she meant well, but enough was enough. "I'm gonna be late for my shift and the new office manager hates that."

"Fine. Lucky for you, she has a soft spot for her family. Thank you." She turned toward the stairway. "Don't forget about Kate's housewarming party."

"I didn't"

Bobby waited for her to climb the stairs before he put his ear protection back in. For the next ten minutes he destroyed his target at the end of the range, only stopping when he ran out of ammo.

The girls weren't wrong. For a guy that never let anything bother him, he'd hit his threshold for being bothered. When he'd left his place to go to work he'd seen Unite Today cult members everywhere he turned. The word had spread fast that he'd shot August Drake.

He didn't imagine they were trying to intimidate him so much as they were documenting his movements to report back to Drake. He expected a visit from him any day now. Bobby rubbed the back of his neck, trying to loosen the muscles. And then there was the whole Theresa situation. He pushed those thoughts aside. Worrying about things he couldn't control wouldn't solve anything.

Finishing up with the hardware, Bobby took the stairs two at a time to talk to Jack before he left for the day. They'd need their own united front to handle Drake and his members.

SETTLING IN HER CHAIR, Cassidy opened the local newspaper and perused the headlines. So far, today had been picture perfect. She woke up to more great reviews for the Brewhouse on social media, had a productive business meeting with the twins, and got things brewing in the brewery. Then she decided to take herself to the best coffee shop in town, Crumbs, for a well-deserved coffee break and something fattening from the pastry case. The piece of apple cinnamon raisin strudel she'd just finished had been divine and worth every calorie. Desserts were something they didn't specialize in at the Brewhouse. Down the road, it would be a good idea to talk shop with Bobby's cousin, Sam, who made the desserts here at Crumbs.

She sipped at her coffee, basking in the warmth radiating from the fireplace, and let it sink in that things were looking up for her. If her mom were here, she'd say that moments like this were few and far between, so you had enjoy them, capture them, then file them away for when the dark days returned. Cassidy refused to count the dark days since her mom had died. Instead she would do just as her mom instructed and relive a filed happy memory of them together.

"You're making this too easy for me."

Cassidy looked up from her paper into the smiling face of her favorite police officer. Huh. Favorite? She hadn't realized she'd chosen

Bobby Maguire as her favorite anything until this moment. He did look wicked hot in his MCPD uniform, all black and tactical like.

"Easy? Well, we can't have that, now can we?"

He sat in the chair to her left in the crowded coffee shop. "How are you, Cassidy?"

"I'm well. How are you AC Maguire?"

"So formal. It's the uniform, right? People always treat me different when I'm dressed for work."

"Maybe it's because you're strapped."

He seemed to like that, his heart-stopping smile breaking across his handsome face.

"Please. Say that again."

"That you're strapped?"

"Yep. Yeah. That's it. That's the one."

She laughed when his eyes rolled back in his head. "Speaking of making it easy."

"Well, I'm not ashamed to admit that it's been awhile."

"Oh? What's that in Bobby Maguire time?" She looked at her watch. "Weeks? Days? Minutes?"

He shook his head. "Don't be like that. I have feelings, too."

One of the Crumb's baristas walked up and handed Bobby a to-go cup.

"You need anything else, Bobby?"

"No thanks, Linda. Have you met my friend, Cassidy?"

"Met? Umm, we went to high school together." With a shake of her head, Linda turned to her. "You good, Cassidy?"

"Yes, thank you," she said before Linda walked back toward the busy counter.

Bobby took a sip from his cup, watching her over the rim, his eyebrows pushed together in confusion. "Why can't I remember you?"

"That's a loaded question."

"Do you look different?"

She shook her head. "Not really."

"Do you come here all the time and I just don't notice you?"

"Yep. I wouldn't rush to take that detective's exam just yet."

"Ouch."

"Right back atcha." Cassidy drank her coffee, enjoying his discomfort. It only hurt a little that he never noticed her.

"How's Brewhouse business?"

"Brilliant. Better than anticipated. Or even hoped for. Slightly exhausting with a hint of Fuck, Yeah!"

"That should be your new advertising slogan."

She nodded. "The twins would love that."

"The twins, huh?" Bobby shifted in his seat. "You seemed pretty cozy with Taylor the other night. Are you dating either of them? Or both? I don't want to be judgmental."

"Both? It would take a woman braver than I to handle a single twin, let alone both, and a woman without a sense of smell. We're just business partners." Cassidy didn't want to read into why he asked, but she did like that he had. "Why? Do you want me to slip one of them a note for you?"

"That's sweet of you to offer, but no, thank you. I just like to have all the facts and the fact is that Taylor seemed a little handsy."

"Handsy?" She couldn't stop her grin. "I should tell him to keep his mitts off then?"

"If you think he's stuck on you, then I'll be happy to tell him to scram."

"I'll keep that in mind."

Bobby sat up straighter in his chair. "On a more serious note, this town has a lot of great restaurants, but by far, that was the best burger I've ever tasted."

"I'll tell the chef you said so."

"Not to mention the beer, which I will mention because it was amazing." He leaned in closer to her. "What else do you recommend I sample?"

"There are so many choices. What do you have a taste for?"

"I enjoy trying all kinds of new things."

She snorted at that. "That's the understatement of the year."

Static broke out on Bobby's police radio, then voices, and he cocked his head toward it so he could listen. He stood, his flirty grin gone. "I've got to go."

Before she could respond, he strode out the coffee shop door. So, that's what it's like to be a small town cop. Here one minute and gone the next. She didn't know what they'd said on the radio or where he might be headed.

She took a deep breath as a thought occurred to her. That's what it would be like to be in a relationship with a small town cop as well. Watching them leave in the middle of a conversation, in the middle of a meal, at all hours of the day or night. She finished her coffee and brought her empty mug up to the counter.

"You don't have to clean up after yourself," Linda said.

"We hard working gals have to stick together. I'm tipping you, too." Cassidy stuck a ten dollar bill in the tip jar on the counter.

"Thank you." Linda took a quick look around. "You open to some free advice to go with that tip?"

Cassidy raised her eyebrows. "Is this where you warn me away from the notorious Bobby Maguire? Honestly, I think he's just sniffing around because he doesn't remember me."

"Maybe. I've probably worked here the longest, so I've seen it all when it comes to Bobby and the women he "dates"." Linda used her fingers to make air quotes.

"Just don't share a number if you have one."

Linda shook her head. "Bobby's changed. A lot. He's here all the time and I've noticed. Sure, he still flirts 'til he's blue in the face, but he's not the player he used to be."

"Are you saying he's finally matured?"

"He is more mature, but something else, too."

"Like what?"

"It's hard to describe. He's definitely more protective of his family and friends with all that has happened here in town. But, he's more – fierce. Like there's something simmering right under the lid all the time."

"Why do you think that?"

"I'm just guessing, but I think he's angry."

"About what?"

"That he can't stop bad things from happening to the people he loves."

A customer walked up capturing Linda's attention. Cassidy headed out the door and strolled to the little parking lot down the block pondering Linda's words. "Fierce," she said to her reflection in her car window. "What would it be like to care for a man who's fierce?"

BOBBY THREW HIS PEN down on his desk and rubbed his eyes with the heels of his hands. He'd left Cassidy hours ago and he was still wrapping up the same case. He hated the overdose calls. Hated that another twenty-something-kid decided shooting up heroin would solve all their problems.

Hated having to notify parents that their child had been found dead with a needle still stuck in their arm. That they'd misjudged the amount, because they were already high. Hated when he knew them. Knew their families. Hated that he'd tried to help them in the past, but they didn't want to stop. Wouldn't stop. Why would they when the next great high was so easy to get?

He hated that this had become so prevalent in his town and he knew they had to put a stop to the flow of drugs, which meant, cutting off access to those drugs. Now that they knew the Cult had contributed to the problem, they were going to have to find a way to shut it down for good.

His fellow officers were all reporting an uptick in sightings of Cult members hanging around Main Street during the day and driving their van around at night. No one had done anything illegal yet. Were they surveilling? Planning? Plotting? All of the above? The phone on his desk buzzed and he picked up the receiver.

"Maguire."

"Why her?"

He recognized Theresa's voice immediately. A part of him wanted to just hang up the phone, but he knew it wouldn't help either of them. He couldn't ignore her any longer. "Theresa? Is that you?" He stalled while he opened the app on his mobile phone to record their conversation.

"Why her?"

"Theresa? Where are you?"

She sniffled. "I hate you."

"Why did you leave that basket with the doll on my door step?"

"You know why. You ruined everything."

"How did I ruin everything? Theresa?"

"I was going to be the one. The one girl that you couldn't live without. You were going to stop seeing all those other women and be mine. It was me. I was going to be the one that changed you. But, now you've got your eye on her!"

"Who?"

"The girl from the bar. Did you think I wouldn't find out about her? That I wouldn't know what you're doing?" Theresa's sniffles were gone, replaced with an angry tone. "Who the hell does she think she is? She doesn't know you. She doesn't get to be with you."

Cassidy. Theresa *had* been at the Brewhouse the other night and she must have seen them talking. Bobby didn't want Theresa's focus to be on Cassidy at all. "She's my friend. But, Theresa, we need to talk about what you're doing. Will you do that? Will you sit down with me and talk this out? Will you please let me help you?"

"You were supposed to love me. But, I don't need anything from you anymore. I've got a new friend. Someone that cares about me and wants to help me."

"Who? Who is helping you, Theresa? Helping you with what?"

She disconnected the call, but not before he heard a man's raised voice in the background. He saved the recording, then hung up the phone. Who the hell had she gotten herself mixed up with?

CHAPTER SIX

Cassidy placed the stainless funnel on the rack and slid it into the commercial dishwasher then shut the door. Wiping her hands on a towel she surveyed the room. Cleanliness was important to making good product. She had scrubbed the whole brew room after finishing a run and before starting another.

Things were looking up. Her projections for how many batches she'd have to make each week had doubled. The twins were already talking about adding more staff so she wouldn't have to tend bar every night after she brewed beer all day.

On her way out to the bar her phone buzzed in her pocket. The screen showed a text from Bobby. A shiver of excitement ran through her. Her drawings were done and he wanted her to come see them at his place after his shift at work.

She hadn't seen him since they'd run into each other at Crumbs, but he'd called the bar the next night to get her personal phone number. He'd texted her a few times. Okay, a lot more than a few. The texts were always friendly. Sometimes flirty. She didn't want to read too much into them. But, she liked it. She liked him. She wouldn't kid herself about how she felt, however, she refused to delude herself into thinking he acted different with her than he did with other women.

"If I had to guess, I would say you're thinking about a man."

Cassidy looked up from her phone to see Bobby's sister, Maggie Maguire, sitting on one of the tall bar stools. She looked just like her campaign photo, on all the posters that hung around town, in her burgundy pants suit and white silk blouse. She had a business planner open in front of her, her phone in one hand, and a glass of water in the other.

"Why would you say that?"

"The emotions crossing your face. You went from happy to completely annoyed in two seconds flat."

"I can't argue with that." She stepped closer to the table. "How are you, Maggie? It's been a while."

"I'm good, thank you. Your Brewhouse has turned out spectacular. Everyone in Maguire's Corner is talking about it. Congratulations."

"Thank you. That's great news. How's your campaign for mayor going?"

"I'll admit, it's not easy running against my own cousin, but I'm getting some great feedback from the community."

"I thought he was your uncle?"

"Technically, he's my father's cousin. Growing up with so much family in the same town, all different ages and tree branches, it gets ... confusing. Sometimes he was Uncle Tom, sometimes he was Cousin Tommy."

"I don't envy you that."

"Speaking of the election, I'm here to talk to you about renting the Brewhouse for election night."

"Really?" Cassidy hadn't expected a job offer.

"Do you have a few minutes to sit down with me?"

"Sure."

Sitting across from Maggie Maguire in a legit business meeting had to be the most bizarre thing Cassidy had done in years. If they could get some positive referrals from clients like her, things could really take off. Trying to look quasi-professional, Cassidy pulled up the notes app on her phone.

"Normally, I would pimp out my own place, Crumbs, to do this sort of thing. But, as you know, the polls close at 9:00 pm and chances are we'll be up for hours after that. I thought it would be nice to loiter in a new venue. One with food and booze."

"That makes sense."

"I'll be out on the street for most of the day, but I think we would need to relocate here around 6:00 pm." She jotted a note in her planner. "I'm thinking buffet style. Appetizers and hot food trays. Open bar, medium shelf."

"How many people would you be expecting?"

Maggie sipped her water then set the glass down. "Conservatively, thirty to forty. Closer to the date I can give you an update on that."

Cassidy tried hard not to make a squee sound. "Of course. Are you going to want to choose specific dishes or have our cooks pick the menu?"

"After what I've heard about the food here, please allow your staff to show off their culinary skills."

"I'll make sure to tell them that. Are you happy having it here in the bar or would you prefer a more private setting?"

"I wasn't aware that you had one available."

"The twins have plans for a game room attached to the bar and two additional rooms that will be available to rent for events. We planned on doing the game one first, but I'm sure they could start on one of the other rooms instead."

"If you think an event room will be done in time, I think that would be perfect. Then you wouldn't lose your bar business for the night."

"It won't be a problem. The plans they drew up had barn door wainscoting, a small corner bar, a big screen TV over a gas fireplace, and small tables to encourage mingling. The boys have a great eye for design. So, how about I speak with them, then write up the notes from our meeting and send it over to you?"

Maggie handed her a business card. "My email's on the back. Cassidy, I've got to say, I'm impressed. And, not just with your Brewhouse."

"Thank you."

"I've got to run." Maggie stood, closed her planner, and slid her phone into her pocket. "Can I ask you one more question?"

"Sure."

"What's his name?"

"Huh?"

"The man that had your emotions on a see saw when I got here?"

"Honestly?" Cassidy stood, returning Maggie's smile. "Your brother."

"Hmm, yes, he can be quite irritating."

"I've hired him to do the artwork for our beer bottle labels."

Maggie sucked in a breath. "And he agreed? To sketch?"

"Yes, in fact he texted to say they were done. I'm going to see them tonight."

"Well, I'll be damned. I can't wait to see what he came up with. Thank you for your time, Cassidy. I'll look for that email from you later today."

"Consider it done."

As Maggie disappeared through the front door, Cassidy finally let out a squee and jumped up and down a few times, catching her phone before she dropped it, and then she ran to find the boys.

"COME ON IN."

Bobby swung the door wide and Cassidy strolled inside his apartment. He helped her take off her olive green field coat then bit his tongue so he didn't whistle when he glimpsed her outfit underneath. He would forever appreciate what a tight brown leather vest could do for a woman's cleavage.

"Thank you, Bobby. It's pretty late. You sure this is okay?"

He hung her coat on a hook near the door. "I'm the one who asked you over. Besides, I just got home from work."

"Are you forced to work at night or are you nocturnally powered?"

"I prefer the late shift most of the time."

She yanked the rubber band from her pony tail, letting the thick waves of her hair fall down around her shoulders. He really dug the purple streaks mixed in with all those black waves. Was that a tattoo peeking out on her waist from under the back of her vest?

He cleared his throat. "Well, let me show you the drawings."

He led her into his spare bedroom and switched on the lights. The room held a large drafting table against the far wall facing the windows and a futon on the left. The rest of the space was taken up with numerous cabinets and standing shelves to hold all of his art supplies. They walked to the table, he turned on the overhead lamp, and she gasped next to him.

"Are these mine? Are these for me?"

"Yeah. There's over a dozen drawings here. Some drawn similar to each other, but maybe from a different angle. I thought you'd like to make the final decisions."

He appreciated that she took her time looking at each page. Some of them she would turn to see better in the light or hold like they were wrapped around a bottle. He'd worked hard on them to prove to himself that he could still get the job done. And, he may have been trying to impress her. It had been a while since a woman had asked more of him than just a good time.

"These are gorgeous. You haven't lost your touch."

"That's kind of you to say. I won't show you the trash bag filled with crumpled rejects."

Cassidy set down the last page. "I love them." She looked around the room. "You acted like you hadn't drawn anything in years and yet you have this whole room set up."

"I enjoy drawing. I just don't spend as much time doing it as I'd like. Most people don't remember that I can."

"I did."

"You did, which still boggles my mind."

She raised her eyebrow. "Did you just use the word boggle in a sentence?"

"Is that some sort of deal breaker?"

"Not for me. I like a man who's secure enough to use his grandfather's colloquiums."

"You're darn tootin'. Stick around. You never know what I might shout out next."

"Hot diggity!"

Bobby laughed and with it went some of his stress from the past few days. He needed to let go a bit. "You – are a very funny gal."

"A day without laughter is a day wasted."

"Quoting Charlie Chaplin?"

"Is that who said it?" She shrugged. "I always thought my mom made it up."

"Here." Bobby pulled out the tall swivel chair for Cassidy to sit down. "So, which ones do you think will work best?"

She sorted through them quickly, splitting them up into two piles. "Definitely, this pile."

"You barely glanced at the ones in the other pile."

She glanced back at him over her shoulder. "I told you, I know what I like when I see it."

That look set his heart racing. "Do you? In all things?"

"Of course."

Giving in to temptation, Bobby threaded his fingers through the ebony strands flowing down her back. He'd never felt anything like it. Soft, yet strong. "Do we even need to do this dance then?"

"This dance?" Cassidy turned the chair until she faced him, forcing him back a step. "You mean the flirting?"

"Flirting? Seems a mild word for what we've been doing."

"I thought it was appropriate."

Bobby crossed his arms over his chest to keep from grabbing her up. "Well, if you haven't progressed beyond flirting to seriously interested, then maybe the dance is still necessary."

She tilted her head. "No, probably not."

Her wicked smile warmed his blood. "I can't tell if you're being serious or not."

"Oh, I never joke about dancing."

"So, when I kiss you, you won't be upset?"

"It would take more than that."

Bobby closed the distance so that her denim clad legs brushed against his thighs. Leaning in, he placed his hands on either side of her, gripping the edge of the table behind her. Her bright silver gaze stayed steady on him. This close he could see her long, dark lashes, and a smattering of light freckles high on her cheekbones.

He advanced slowly, prolonging the moment, unsure how she would react, yet she blindsided him, meeting him half way. Her lush lips under his made time stand still. Everything froze around him, yet inside, everything sped up. His blood roared through his veins, his heart threatening to beat from his chest.

Her fingers closed over the neck of his shirt, pulling him closer. She opened her mouth, letting him in, her tongue teasing against his, deepening the kiss. She tasted as exotic as she looked, like cinnamon and sin, and he was starving. With a gentle nudge of his leg, her knees parted and he stepped between them, bringing their bodies closer.

Cassidy nipped his bottom lip sending a bolt of desire straight through him. The palms of her hands slid down his chest leaving hot trails through his T-shirt. His senses were overwhelmed and a hunger for her spread through him. He wanted her and he needed her to know it. He released the table so he could hold on to her. Gripping her hips, he rocked his body against hers. She broke their kiss on a gasp.

"Bobby."

He moved in to taste her again, but she turned her head, exposing her neck. He kissed a path to her earlobe, then pulled the delicate flesh into his mouth. Her body trembled against his, her hands gripping his arms.

She groaned. "Hot damn, that's nice."

"I couldn't agree more."

He captured her lips again in a slow, deep, mind-blowing kiss while he slid his hands from her hips to her waist, below her vest, to touch her bare skin. A powerful ache for this woman rose inside him, and yet, even in a haze of need he recognized her two hands pushing against his chest and he reluctantly ended their kiss.

"We should stop."

He eased back. "I couldn't agree less. Why?"

She took a few deep breaths which didn't help as he watched her breasts rise and fall beneath her vest.

"Because, this is a little fast for me."

"We can go any speed you like."

"And, I'm well aware of your reputation."

Her hands fell to her lap when he stepped away. "My reputation?"

"I'm sure you know you have one."

He scrubbed his hand over his hair, his brain still foggy. "Is this you playing hard to get?"

"Don't misunderstand. I'm completely interested. But, I'm not going to sleep with you tonight just because you're a really good kisser."

Bobby shrugged. "Does my reputation include that I've never led a woman on? I enjoy women. I enjoy sex. I'm not interested in relationships."

"Yes, I'm aware of that. However, I do think we're both worth more than a quick roll in the hay." She stood, slipping by him to the doorway. "Thank you, Bobby, for all your hard work. I want the drawings in the stack on the right. Email me the invoice and I'll get you a check."

CHAPTER SEVEN

The hum of desire still ran through Cassidy's whole body and she needed to leave Bobby's apartment fast or make a total fool of herself and jump him where he stood. He knew precisely how to kiss a girl until she forgot her own name and address. Now, she understood how he could talk so many women into bed, without talking at all.

She headed toward his front door, Bobby close behind.

"Cassidy?"

She stopped at the door, turning to face him. "Yes?"

"I don't think of you like that. Like a quick roll in the hay."

"That's good to know."

Not an admission of true feelings, but it was a start. Building a little anticipation would do them both some good. She smiled at the look on his face, like smoldering confusion. She took her coat from him, tying the arms around her waist. Her overheated body would keep her warm all the way home.

"Night, Bobby."

"Night, Cassidy."

He opened the door and with a goofy grin she couldn't shake Cassidy ambled down his sidewalk, toward the parking lot. A burst of white light filled her vision, blinding her, and an angry roar sounded in front of her. She lifted her arms to shield herself. A stinging pain flared on her wrist and Cassidy's nose filled with the coppery smell of blood and the bitterness of beer.

"Cassidy!"

No matter how many times she blinked her eyes she still couldn't see. She heard footsteps behind her, then strong hands gripped her shoulders, pulling her back.

"Get behind me."

"Bobby?" Her heart beat heavy in her chest.

"I've got you. We're walking back to my front steps."

"I can't see anything." He held her close to him, keeping her from tripping.

"Just take a seat on the steps. I'll be right back. I need to grab a towel for your arm."

"Wait!" She grabbed at his arms. "I can't see."

"I know, but you're bleeding."

"What happened? Who was that?" What the hell was going on? Why couldn't she see?

"It's okay. You're okay. It was a high-intensity flashlight. The effects will wear off. Just keep your eyes closed for a bit. I need to wrap up your arm."

He brushed by her as he went in the house. She took a few deep breaths, keeping her eyes shut.

"I'm back." Bobby lifted her injured arm. "I'm going to wrap a towel around this cut and then I'm taking you to the ER. You're gonna need stitches."

"Bobby, who hit me? What's going on?" She sucked in a breath when he pulled the towel tight.

"I'm sorry, Cassidy. It was that girl you met at the Brewhouse, Theresa. She flashed that light in your face and then hit you with a beer bottle."

"Why?"

"I guess she didn't think three dates were enough."

"You dated her? Has she done stuff like this before?"

"Hold on to me." He helped her stand.

"So, like, you have your very own stalker?"

"Time to go."

Cassidy didn't need her vision to read between the lines. Bobby's non-answers were telling her everything she needed to know.

"Do we have to go to the hospital? We can't just use some gauze?"

"It looks pretty deep. You should get checked out by someone more qualified than me. There could be glass in it, too."

Cassidy held tightly to Bobby as he led her to the parking lot. The smell of real leather seats made her realize they were getting into his Mustang.

"Don't let me get blood all over your car, Bobby."

"That's the last thing I care about right now." The sound of the car starting gave her goosebumps. "The heat should kick on in a minute. I've got to call this in to my boss. I'll be just outside the car."

Cassidy opened her eyes and breathed a sigh of relief. Her eyesight was blurry, but returning. Warm air blew from the vents onto her shaking limbs. Shaking because she'd been attacked by Bobby's stalker, Theresa. Is that why she came to the Brewhouse? To follow Bobby? To see what he did, who he spoke to? Now she knew why Theresa had given her such a bad vibe.

Bobby slid in behind the wheel. "How are you doing? Are you okay?"

"Yeah. My vision is blurry, but that's better than before. My arm is starting to throb, though."

He put the car in gear and pulled out of the lot. "I'm sorry, Cassidy."

"Tell me about Theresa. What happened?"

Bobby downshifted for a stop sign and then made a left onto the road that would take them to the hospital. This car was meant for speed, but he drove slowly through the dark streets.

"She's a problem that I should have taken care of, but didn't."

"You never told anyone she was bothering you?"

"No. I guess I figured if I ignored her, she'd eventually go away. I never thought she'd hurt someone else."

Cassidy looked over at Bobby. Anger radiated off of him like waves. Linda's use of the word 'fierce' repeated in her head.

"Someone else? Does that mean she's hurt you?"

Bobby cleared his throat. "Heads up about the ER. My cousin Kate is most likely working and if you don't know about her then let me just say that nothing in your life will ever be private again."

"I do know Kate. Don't worry. I won't say anything."

"That won't matter."

Bobby pulled into the hospital parking lot and parked his car behind the police chief's truck. He came around to the passenger side to help her out. The sliding doors opened as they approached the ER and they walked inside to see Doctor Kate Maguire standing next to Jack Munro in front of a large counter.

"AC Maguire."

"Chief. Kate. This is Cassidy."

Even with Bobby standing right next to her, she could acknowledge the formidable cop in front of her took her breath away. Considering how many handsome men she knew, that would be a tall order.

She didn't mind taking a good long look at him either. She'd seen the chief many times, but never had the opportunity to meet him. Never had those striking eyes assess her from head to toe. But, she much preferred Bobby's warm inviting, mischievous brown eyes on her than the chief's icy blue stare.

"Cassidy. I'm Chief Jack Munro. I'll be taking your statement after you get treated."

"My statement?"

"For the assault charges. Why don't you go with Dr. Maguire to get checked out while I speak with AC Maguire?"

Kate led her to an open curtained area while the men walked down the hall. Cassidy already missed the warmth of Bobby's hand on her back.

"It's been a while, Cassidy, but I remember you from school. I'm sorry we have to meet again under these circumstances."

"It's nice to see you, Kate."

"Take a seat and we'll get you all fixed-up." Kate walked to the sink to wash her hands.

"Thank you." Sitting down heavily, Cassidy tried to compose herself. She hadn't been back in this hospital since her mother had passed. It smelled the same. Like bleach and old flowers with an underlying tinge of death.

"Any idea what you were cut with?"

"Bobby said it was a beer bottle. Honestly, after the light flashed in my eyes, everything is pretty confusing."

Kate moved a cart of supplies closer to the bed. After donning a pair of purple gloves she slowly un-wrapped the towel. "We will definitely check your vision then, too."

Cassidy bit her lip when Kate started to poke around in the wound, but she followed Kate's directions during the rest of her exam.

"So, it's not as deep as it is long and, lucky for you, it's not where all the important bits are located. Still, it's going to take a few stitches to get this jagged mess closed up neatly. I'm going to have the nurse get some information from you and clean out this cut, then I'll be back to stitch it. Okay?"

"Yeah, okay. Thank you."

"And then, you can tell me all about what you were doing over at Bobby's apartment in the middle of the night and why someone attacked you."

CHAPTER EIGHT

"Dammit, Bobby. How long has this been going on?"

Bobby steeled himself for Jack's anger, hating that his boss had found out this way. He'd put off telling him for so long, and so much had occurred, it seemed so much worse now.

"A couple of months." Jack's silent disapproval hung heavy on Bobby's shoulders. His own regret seeped right down to his bones. "I'm sorry, Chief."

"I don't know what you were thinking. How could you not tell me about this? I thought after all this time that you at least trusted me."

"It's not that…"

"It's exactly that." Jack threw his hands in the air. "You and your sister. Unbelievable."

"I thought I could handle the situation myself."

"Why? Why would you have to handle anything by yourself when you have the entire police department backing you up?"

Bobby crossed his arms over his T-shirt feeling underdressed talking to his boss without his uniform on. "I'm not sure that's accurate."

"What does that even mean?"

"I'm aware of my reputation in this town, Jack. Some of the people here might think I deserved it. That maybe I brought it on myself."

"No one deserves to have a crazy person disrupt their entire life. And, that still doesn't explain why you completely disregarded coming to me as your boss. As your friend."

"Well, maybe I thought you'd be disappointed in me if I couldn't handle it on my own."

Jack shook his head. "Next time think about what I'll do to you if you don't tell me what's going on before I have to meet you in the ER." He took out his pad and pen. "How many people knew Cassidy would be at your house tonight?"

"Just us, I thought. I had texted her earlier in the evening asking her to come over when she was done with work."

"What happened tonight?"

"Cassidy was leaving. I was still in my doorway, watching her walk to her vehicle. She was half way down the sidewalk when the brightest light I've ever seen turned on right in front of her. I looked down to avoid the light and then I heard glass breaking and a shout. I moved forward and as I reached Cassidy I grabbed her and moved her back, behind me. When I looked around she was already gone."

"And by 'she' you mean Theresa?"

Bobby rubbed the back of his neck. "Yes."

"If you didn't see her, how do you know Theresa attacked Cassidy?"

"I couldn't see her, but I heard her. The shout was definitely her. I shouldn't even call it a shout. It was like a rage-filled scream."

"So, either Theresa was watching your place and saw Cassidy go in and took the opportunity to attack her when she came out or she was coming after you tonight."

"It's possible."

"Okay. Let's back up. When did all this start?"

"Right." Bobby turned his head side to side, his neck still tight, and then blew out a breath before he shared his story. "End of June or so I asked Theresa out for drinks. A few days later we went out for dinner then went back to her place. By our third date she was already making plans about us cohabitating."

"How so?"

"I went to pick her up, but when I get there she says she's changed her mind about going out. She invites me in and she's got a romantic dinner for two all set in her living room. I excuse myself to use the restroom and I find some of my things on the bathroom counter. I start checking around and she's either taken my stuff from my place or bought the same products and brands that I use and has them all over her apartment. I confront her about it and she lost it. Destroys the dinner and starts throwing things at me, screaming for me to leave."

"Did you?"

"Of course, right after I made it clear we were done. I gave her the usual speech. I was never looking for anything long-term and that I had no interest in pursuing anything further with her."

"How long before you noticed there was an issue?"

Bobby crossed his arms again. "About a week later the phone calls start. Text messages. She left notes on my car. In my mailbox. One morning I find her in my kitchen. She's got dinner recreated on my table, right down to the vegetables. I tell her to leave before I have to charge her with trespassing. That's the day I got cut with the wine glass."

"The day you told me you tripped and fell?"

"Yes."

"But you didn't fall, she assaulted you. She cut you with the wine glass and you got how many stitches?"

"I don't recall. A few."

Jack stared at him for a long moment and Bobby held still, refusing to squirm under that piercing gaze.

"She's the one who scratched up your car, too. Isn't she?"

"Yes, that was her."

"Son of a ...." Jack shook his head. "I can't wait to read your full, honest, don't leave a word out, report about this entire disaster and I assume you've kept any evidence?"

"Everything's in the trunk of my car."

"Everything? Because there's a lot?"

"Yes. I have photos on my phone and backups on my laptop. I have a computer file documenting every incident."

"Of course you do. I would have fired you if you didn't."

Bobby waited quietly while Jack wrote his notes. The tension level had dropped some, but he knew the wrong word from him could blow it.

Jack put away his pen and pad. "Now, tell me about Cassidy."

"What about her?"

"Who is she to you? Why was she at your place?"

"She's a friend. She hired me to do the artwork for the beer labels at the Brewhouse. We've been working together on it and she came over tonight to see the final drawings."

"That's it?"

"For now." Jack raised his eyebrow and Bobby found himself fighting not to squirm again. "What?"

"You tell me."

"I find her interesting. Maybe a little mysterious."

"Well, you just left her with the town gossip. You'll know everything there is to know about her in about ten minutes."

"Cassidy's pretty savvy. I'm not sure even Kate could get info out of her."

"I TOLD HER EVERYTHING."

"You what?"

Bobby sat on the edge of the ER bed by Cassidy's feet. She had a thick white bandage wrapped around her left forearm. Guilt stabbed him in the gut. He added the dark circles under her eyes to his list of things to take the blame for. Cassidy would never have gotten hurt if he'd only reported Theresa's actions earlier.

"I didn't mean to. Kate just started to stitch my arm, asked me if I was okay, and then I told her everything."

"Everything, everything?" He looked all around them and then leaned in closer. "Like about ...what happened between us earlier tonight everything?"

"Pretty much."

"Shit."

She shook her head. "How does she do it?"

"No one knows. If she weren't related, I'd have her strung up as a witch." He let out a small laugh at the look on Cassidy's face. "I'm kidding. A little. Let's worry about that later. Are you okay?"

"My vision is back to normal. Kate said that if I keep my arm clean and dry I can have the stiches out in ten days or so."

"That's good. Have I mentioned how sorry I am?"

"Not in the last hour, no."

"I'm really sorry."

"I'm not blaming you. Besides, I'm putting a positive spin on this whole situation. I'm figuring I saved you from your stalker."

"You're my hero?"

"Exactly."

Looking at Cassidy, her eyes lit with laughter, her smile wide across her face, something shifted inside Bobby's chest, like a heavy door trying to open. Warmth, like he'd never known, shone through the gap. Before he could catch a glimpse of what might be waiting inside for him, he mentally slammed the door shut. The timing couldn't have been worse. He had a good thing going here. No use muddying it up with unwanted emotions.

Cassidy tilted her head. "Hey? Where'd you go?"

"Sorry. I was just thinking." Bobby stood. "I'm thankful it wasn't worse."

"Will they arrest Theresa?"

"Yes. They're out looking for her now. Jack is waiting to take your statement."

"And, she'll get some help?"

He nodded. "Help will be available, but she'll have to want help."

"You sound pretty angry."

"I'm not sure anger covers how I feel about her. She's done enough damage. It's time for this to end. Let's go talk to Jack so I can take you home."

CHAPTER NINE

Cassidy trudged up the stairs to her loft apartment. Living above her job had its pros and cons and being steps from her bed after an exhausting day would definitely be in the pro column. Her cold, lonely bed. Well, it didn't have to be cold or lonely if she didn't want it to be. She knew a guy who'd help her out with that.

Thinking about Bobby warmed her inside and out. It had been so long since their kiss, she'd started to think she'd imagined it. But, she could remember every single second of that kiss. Every detail. Every lip-smacking moment. He'd invited her over tonight to watch a movie after work, but between the long day on her feet brewing and the long evening on her feet serving she'd have to pass.

Wrapping up her bandaged arm in plastic, she managed a quick shower, then pulled on sweats and a t-shirt. Readying the supplies she'd picked up at the drug store, she cut off the old gauze and checked her wound. Kate was an artist. Her stitches were so tiny and so close together, Cassidy didn't think she'd have much of a scar to show off. She followed the steps the nurses had shown her the other day. Carefully clean, apply antibiotic, re-wrap with gauze.

She curled up on her cozy 'chair and a half', one of only two pieces of furniture in her spacious living room. She grabbed her mobile phone from the coffee table and found two texts from Bobby. The first one let her know that he had arrived home from his shift and the second just had a question mark.

Should she feel giddy he showed interest in her knowing she would be another notch on his bed post? Could she trust a man like that? Of course, she'd have to go to bed with him first before she claimed a notch position. Imagining sex with Bobby gave her chills. Reliving the minutes in his art room had her blushing like a teen. His mouth on hers and his hands, good gracious those hands.

Okay. So, she had the same hormone riddled blood running through her veins like all his other women. That didn't make her a bad person. A naïve woman would think they could change a man, make them better. Cassidy didn't want to change Bobby, she just wanted to sleep with him. Only, she didn't have all his – experience. She'd need a little time.

"If you're calling me that must mean that you're not coming over."

Bobby's voice surprised the crap out of her. She'd accidentally pressed the call button? She quickly lifted the phone to her ear. "Hey. Yeah, I'm sorry, but I'm pretty wiped out."

"I get it. How's your arm? Is it getting better?"

"It's healing up nice. Just a couple more days until the stitches come out."

"Good. I'm glad to hear that. Did you make beer today?"

"I did. Lots of it. Then I worked the bar."

"Ah, brewmaster and beer wench. No wonder you're tired. If you were here, I'd rub your feet."

Cassidy smiled, wiggling her own toes. A foot rub sounded decadent. "Are you trying to bribe me?"

"If I thought it would work."

"You'll need more than pampering promises to get me in the car tonight."

"Name it."

"Stop. You're not that desperate."

"I can't tell, was that insult for me or for you?"

She shifted in her chair. Her mother's voice echoed in her head reminding her to accept compliments and use her manners. "Sorry."

"If it makes it easier, I'll tell you the same thing that I tell any woman I'm attracted to. I'm not interested in a long-term relationship.

I just want to have some fun, enjoy each other's company, and if no one gets attached, no one gets hurt."

"How incredibly romantic. You actually get women into bed with that line?"

His rumble of laughter made her smile. "I've had some success, yes."

"Well, I'm not going to hop into your bed cause that's where you want me."

"I can think of quite a few places that I want you."

Did his voice drop down an octave? Cassidy fanned her warm face. "Good. I like a man who's inventive."

"But not one that's impatient."

"Are you? Impatient? For me?" That popped out of her mouth without being screened. She held her breath waiting for his response.

"Does that please you?"

"Yes."

"Tell me why."

Cassidy got up from her chair and headed to one of the small windows that overlooked a nearby corn field. His question didn't have an easy answer. "Girls like it when a guy shows interest."

"Nope. Try again."

"Because." She sighed trying to find the words. "Sometimes I look at you, and you look so good I can barely breathe."

"I like the sound of that."

"I don't want to be the only one that feels that way." She paced to the other end of the room. "You can have any girl."

"Clearly, not any girl. You're the girl I want."

"At the moment."

"True. But, that's what you want too, right? Nothing serious?"

"Sure." The conversation made her head spin. She wandered back to her chair and flopped down on it. "Exactly. No muss, no fuss."

"I'm interested in you. It's not the chase."

"Ha!"

"Okay, it's not *just* the chase. I like you."

Her finger knotted in her hair and she shook it loose. "I like you, too."

"Good. Then you can stop questioning my motives."

The sound of him moving had her curious. Was he on the couch? Would he watch a movie without her? Did he make popcorn?"

"Cassidy?"

"Yes?"

"What are you wearing?"

Laughing out loud, she stood, moving back to the window. "So smooth."

"You laughed."

"You are some kind of funny."

"Okay. Let's get serious for a minute. Tell me one thing about yourself that you never told anyone else."

"You want a secret?" She wandered into her kitchen to forage. Serious secret talk required serious chocolate.

"Not like a confession, but something you don't share with just anyone."

"Will this admission be reciprocated?"

"You want a secret from me?"

"Desperately. And, something good, not like where you slept with all your conquests." Finding a bag of semi-sweet baking chips in the cabinet, she ripped it open, spilling some on the counter.

"Fine. I'll show you mine, after you show me yours."

"A secret. Okay. Let me think. Can't share that. No. Maybe that? No, better not."

"Come on. Share something."

"I may have body art."

"I believe I saw part of a tattoo on your body the other day."

"You saw one of them."

"Very intriguing and yet I already know about it."

"Okay, okay, I've got one, but this is not for you to repeat. Ever."

"Promise."

She ate a few chips for courage. "College. I was always running short on money for stuff I needed, like food. Waitressing was good, but it wasn't cutting it. So, I had to make a risqué decision."

"Will I have to recuse myself from this conversation?"

"No, nothing illegal. Nothing like that. Chief."

"Nice touch."

"Some girls I knew danced at a club part-time for extra cash, but I've been told I look like I'm having a seizure on the dance floor. And, that whole pole thing? Not as easy as the ladies make it look."

"Duly noted."

Cassidy looked down to see she'd eaten all the loose chips off the counter. "Then I saw an ad for nude models for the local art school."

"No way."

"Way. I sat nude for art students."

"Like one time?"

"Four or five semesters total. The teachers would switch subjects now and then, so I'd have to wait for my turn again."

"Naked, naked?"

"Completely."

"Holy. Crap." He made some kind of groaning noise that had her fanning her face again. "So, college guys-"

"And girls."

"Even hotter. College guys and girls would stare at your naked body for an hour while drawing your parts in their sketchbooks?"

"You make it sound so seedy."

"I may need to excuse myself."

"Oh, no you don't. You owe me a secret." She left the open bag of chips on the counter, heading back for her chair.

"You can't expect me to get over that story so quickly."

"Well, I do."

"I'm still thinking about you, in all your nakedness, poised on the chaise lounge."

She stopped in the middle of her living room. "How did you know there was a chaise lounge?"

"It may have been brief, but I was an art student. I've drawn a few naked girls in my time and there's always a chaise lounge involved."

"I'm sure. Okay. No more changing the subject, it's your turn."

"Right. Secret."

She flopped back down and swung her legs over the arm of the chair. "Something good."

"Okay. Fine. Here's my big secret, but it's not nearly as interesting as yours. I could have graduated high school when I was 16, but I stayed so my friends wouldn't make fun of me."

"16? You were a junior?"

"Sophomore, actually."

"Huh. Are you some kind of genius?"

"Hardly. I'm just able to memorize lots of information very easily and that made school surprisingly effortless for me."

"But, you didn't want your friends to know that?

"Not really. I had enough to deal with being a Maguire. Being Robert Maguire's son. The other kids already thought I got special treatment."

"Did you?"

"No. Dad always told me that you can't control what people think so don't try."

She'd always thought he'd had it so easy during school, but he had his demons to deal with, too. "Huh."

"I hope you don't let this information change your opinion of me."

"Not the way you think. It's kind of hot. I might make you put on a pair of glasses and talk nerdy to me."

"Oh? Does that do it for you?"

"Lots of things do it for me."

"Really? Like what?"

She smiled at his eagerness to know. "You told me I was making it too easy for you, so I guess you'll just have to find out the hard way."

There was a long pause on his end before he said, "Challenge accepted."

CHAPTER TEN

Bobby stopped for coffee at Crumbs before his shift started. They were busy at the counter so he sat at one of the tall tables to wait. He couldn't stop the onslaught of yawns that overtook him.

"Looks like I brought this to you just in time."

Maggie set a large cup in front of him then sat in the chair to his right. Bobby reached into his pants pocket for his bottle of aspirin, shaking three into his palm. He removed the lid from the to-go cup and swallowed the pills down with huge gulps of the hot coffee.

"Looks like. Thanks, Mags."

"You're welcome. How are things with you?"

He snorted. Her interrogations always started out so friendly. "Fine. And you?"

"I'm well, thank you. It seems like I haven't seen you in forever."

"Or, at least a few hours."

"Days, if we're being honest." Maggie crossed her legs and smoothed down her skirt. "So, why don't you fill me in?"

"Why? By now you've spoken to Jack and Kate. You know more about what's going on in my life than I do."

"But, I want to hear it from you."

He rubbed his forehead, wishing the pills would kick in faster. "Are we really doing this?"

"Of course we are. You didn't think this coffee was free, did you?" She smiled at him. "Theresa Wallace?"

"Stalker. Stay away from her. There's a warrant out for her arrest."

"Unite Today?"

"Dangerous. Do not engage with any of their members."

"Jack?"

"Pissed." He sighed. "I'm not sure how to fix that one."

"Pizza and beer, probably."

"It may not be that easy."

"Give him a little time." Maggie sipped her coffee. "Cassidy from the Brewhouse?"

He paused, flashing back to their kiss, the one that had nearly brought him to his knees. "What about her?"

"That's all I needed to hear."

"Stop making assumptions. Now, I need information from you. Why don't I remember Cassidy from high school?"

Maggie set down her cup. "Because she didn't walk around the halls with her boobs hanging out and she didn't throw herself into your lap at every opportunity."

"Besides that."

"No really. You were that shallow and didn't notice girls like Cassidy. Now you're older and can appreciate real beauty when it's standing in front of you."

"Wow."

"It's true and you know it. Why don't you tell *me* about Cassidy?"

He thought about dodging his sister's question, but the words were out of his mouth before he could change the subject. "I like her."

"Hand me a pen, I need to write this down."

"Shut up or I'm leaving."

Maggie held up her hands in mock surrender. "Okay, okay. What else?"

"She's different. Funny. Real."

"That's important."

"I just can't understand why I don't recognize her."

"Well, she's only been around since high school. She moved to town with her mom just before her freshman year began."

"Ah, so only a few years. What else?"

"She wasn't terribly outgoing, but not a wallflower either. She probably didn't hit your radar cause she wasn't into sports or in any of your advanced classes. That's about all I remember. She lost her mom recently. Cancer, I think."

"She mentioned that. Nothing about her dad, though."

"No, I don't think I know anything about her father. Maybe Kate would know more."

Bobby drained his cup. "Are we done with your interrogation yet?"

"We used to call it 'catching up.'"

"That was mom & dad's catch phrase for digging into my business. Now, between you, Emily, and Kate, I have no privacy at all."

She shrugged. "You're lucky I didn't sic mom on you."

"She's got no power over me."

"Bullshit!"

He gasped for effect. "This is how our new mayor speaks? Such a potty mouth."

"Don't jinx me."

"Come on. Do you really think anyone in our family will vote Uncle Tom over you?"

"I refuse to speculate. By the way, I booked the Brewhouse for election night. Cassidy said the twins are working on the event room already and it should be done in plenty of time."

"You got to her, too? Can't anything be just for me?"

"Wow. Those words are very telling."

Bobby groaned. "You read into everything, Maggie. I've got to go."

"Okay. Oh, but you should bring Cassidy to Kate's housewarming party."

He'd actually already thought about asking Cassidy, but family events were dangerous territory to bring an unsuspecting girl, especially his family. "And drop her into the lion's den? Are you crazy?" He stood and pushed his chair back in.

"We're not that bad."

"Individually, not so bad. It's when the Maguires are all together that chaos ensues. Thanks for the coffee."

CHAPTER ELEVEN

Driving to a crime scene at the local cemetery in the month of October had to be one of the creepiest things Bobby had ever done. At this early hour the fog hadn't burned off all the way making the trip extra spooky. Dry leaves swept down the road, spun by an unseen hand. Bobby shivered. He'd managed to scare himself.

Bobby arrived as the chief exited his own truck. The fall air was crisp so he put on his MCPD coat over his uniform. His cousin, Emily, stood on the side of the dirt road, bundled in a sweatshirt two sizes too big for her. He grabbed his notebook and joined them. He gave her a quick hug noting how her hands shook slightly and her eyes appeared a little glazed.

"You okay, Emily?"

"No. I discovered a body this morning on my walk."

Jack pulled out his pad and pen while looking around the graveyard. "Do I need to state the obvious?"

"I know what you're thinking, but this one's – fresh. Well, from the smell, it's not that fresh." She shivered. "Anyway, there's a body on the floor of the Hunt family mausoleum."

"And, you're here at this hour because?" Bobby had a pretty good idea why, but Jack had taught him to let the witness respond to the questions, not to assume the answers.

"I take walks through here a lot."

"You always walk off the main path this far?"

"Sometimes."

Bobby turned his head to look over at Avery's plot which wasn't far from where they were standing. "You know why we're asking."

"I'm fine, guys. I do visit Avery's grave quite often. I'm not living in the past or anything, I'm just being respectful."

Jack flipped open his pad. "What made you notice the Hunt mausoleum?"

"It's on my way back out and I saw the gate was kind of leaning to one side. I walked up the path to take a closer look. Not only is the gate broken, but the vault door is open about six inches. I didn't touch anything, just tried to catch a glimpse. I'd thought maybe an animal had died inside, but it's a person. One really dead person."

"Thank you, Emily." Jack closed his pad and stuck it in his jacket pocket. "I can have an officer take you home."

"I'd like to stay if that's okay. I'm completely grossed out already, so I might as well watch you guys work."

"That's fine. Just stand clear of the scene. Bobby, let's get started."

The heavy, creaking sound the door made when they pried it the rest of the way open fit right in with the rest of Bobby's spooky, hair-raising narrative. There, in the middle of the floor, a body lay face down. He worked closely with the crime scene unit as they photographed, catalogued, and measured everything in and around the crypt. When the techs were satisfied, they moved on to the body, which they'd been referring to as 'she' because of the victim's clothing and long hair.

After the preliminary exam, photos, and trace evidence had been collected they were ready to turn her over. Bobby had been writing notes when Emily gasped from the doorway. He looked at the body and a shudder ran through him. Even with discolored skin and covered in blood he could easily identify the woman.

"Emily? Do you recognize this person?" Jack's voice echoed in the stone room.

"It's Theresa Wallace."

A slice across her neck stretched from ear to ear and now that they had moved her, more dark blood oozed from the glistening ragged wound. Bobby's last cup of coffee swirled dangerously around in his gut. He'd never contaminated a crime scene, but he thought he might actually hurl at the gruesome picture before him.

What the hell happened? Who could do this? He looked up from the sickening sight to Jack who stood directly opposite him. His boss lifted his gaze from the body and pinned those penetrating eyes on him.

"AC Maguire, can you confirm this is Theresa Wallace?"

"I can. It is."

"Do we have time of death yet?" Jack asked the room in general.

One of the techs responded. "We're still waiting for the coroner to arrive, but by the looks of things, the body hasn't been in here more than twenty-four hours."

"AC Maguire, why don't you head outside and see what's keeping the coroner."

"Yes, sir."

With one last look at the body Bobby walked out of the Hunt mausoleum. He would never forget the frozen look of terror on Theresa's face. Or the copious amounts of blood on her skin, in her hair, pooling under her body.

Bobby's brain buzzed with questions. Her clothes. She wore her waitress uniform under a parka which meant she was either on her way to work or on her way home. Not through the cemetery though. She lived on the other end of town. She always drove to work, so where's her car? Who had she run in to? Who would do this to her? After he called the coroner, he wrote down all his observations and questions. No matter what she'd done, he'd find her killer.

MANAGING FULL GARBAGE bags in one hand and some recycles in the other, Cassidy made it out the Brewhouse kitchen door without dropping anything. She waited for the motion sensor lights to turn on, but they didn't notice her. Even waving the empty plastic bottles in the air got her nothing. Another thing to tell the twins. Change the angle for her normal height instead of their freakishly tall bodies.

Her eyes adjusted to the dim light and she made her way down the back of the building. She deposited all the items into the dumpster and recycle cans. Wiping her hands on her pants she turned around and the lights flared to life, flooding her still sensitive vision. She lifted her arm to shield her face and blinked rapidly.

"Hello, Cassidy."

She recognized that voice and she took a large step back as the shape of a man appeared before her.

"Drake."

"I didn't mean to startle you."

"Well, you did." A few deep breaths helped slow her racing heart. "The irony of you slumming out by the garbage is not lost on me."

He moved to her side so she lowered her arm. Drake towered over her, with his wide shoulders and long legs. His hair had been buzzed short recently, the blonde appearing almost white against his weathered skin.

"I need to talk to you."

"Did you ban telephones up at Cult-Town?"

"I wanted to see you in person."

"And now you have." Bits of her buried anger surfaced in his presence. Words she swore she'd never say to him came rising to the top. "You're just a few months late. You missed mom's funeral."

He crossed his massive arms, a sure sign he meant to intimidate her. She knew all his tells. "I wasn't able to attend your mother's service. I had business"

"Excuses, excuses. You have them for everything."

"You sure got your momma's smart mouth."

Sweat broke out across her body as she remembered fights between Drake and her mother beginning just like this. They always ended with him smacking her mother across the face. Until the day he hit Cassidy. "What do you want?"

"There's been some trouble. Your brother, August, is in the hospital. He's been shot."

"Is he going to live?"

"He was shot in the knee. He'll never walk normal again."

"Well, let's be frank, he wasn't normal to begin with. Who shot him? One of his thug friends? A rival cult member?"

"Your local police. My lawyer is drawing up papers to sue the MCPD and Assistant Chief Maguire as we speak."

"Bobby? Why?"

He stared at her, his silver-grey eyes boring into her own. "Maguire pulled the trigger." He lowered his arms, shoving his hands deep into his pockets. "I came to talk to you about moving back home. Your mother is no longer an impediment. You need to return to where you belong."

She shook her head before he finished his sentence, her temper spiking at his careless comment. "Did you add recreational pharmaceuticals to your fruit punch? We didn't leave the compound because of her, we left because of you. Besides, I've never belonged up there."

"Every day this town gets more dangerous and the ones that should be protecting us are the ones that put us in harm's way. We've made a good life for ourselves at Unite Today, a safe life. One where you don't get randomly attacked on the sidewalk."

His comment landed like a punch to the stomach. He stared at her arm with the bandage on it. "How did you know that?"

"There's very little in this town that I don't know."

"I see. The Membership Watch. The cult members are still spying for you. They see all and report back every little thing."

"They tell me that you've been going to Maguire's residence. More than once. They tell me that's where you were attacked."

Waves of animosity poured off of him and she had to fight not to take another step back.

"That's what this visit is really all about? You found out that I've been talking to the cop that shot your idiot son, who was probably doing something illegal at the time, and you want me to what? Talk to him? Get him to see reason?"

"No. Come back home. Join us. We don't take kindly to those that hurt our kin. We're not the criminals. Look to your politicians for the real source of corruption. They've made the first strike against us. We'll fight them all, side by side, as a family."

The hostility behind his words scared her to the core. "Let's get this straight. The only family I ever had, died a few months ago from cancer. I have no interest in your politics or your eccentric hostile way of life. I'll never come back to your Cult."

Once again he looked at her long and hard. "Strong words, Cassidy." With a small nod he walked by her, the way he'd come. "Let's hope you never regret them."

A chill shook her body and not just from the crisp air. Drake and the Cult had always been kind of a joke, but she'd just witnessed how a single action could turn idiots into a dangerous enemy. She should tell someone. She should tell Bobby, however that discussion came with a can of worms she had no interest in opening. She walked toward the back door and the lights went out, causing her to jump.

She bolted for the back door handle and ran inside only to get grabbed up the moment she entered the hallway that led to the bar. Her fight reflexes kicked in and she struggled against the hands that held her.

"Whoa, whoa, it's me. It's Bobby."

Relief poured through her and she slumped against his chest, loving the way his arms stole around her, holding her close, feeling just right.

"Hey, what happened? Are you okay?"

She nodded her head against him, his warmth chasing away the chill she'd just experienced. Bobby released her and she moved back. "I'm fine. I thought I saw something outside when those stupid sensor lights just suddenly turned off."

Were words even coming out of her mouth right? Did the man have to look this damn good dressed in his MCPD uniform? Every solid inch in black. All badass and hot. Those deep brown eyes scanning her. She resisted the urge to rush back into his arms.

"What are you doing here?"

"I'm on a break. They told me you were back here and I figured I'd say hello." He looked up and down the hallway then inched closer to her. "In private."

A badass cop that wanted to see her in private? Her day was looking up. "Who am I to argue?"

Bobby flashed a grin before he grabbed her up again to kiss her soundly. She wound her arms around his shoulders. While he ravaged her mouth, his hands repeated the same alluring pattern on her body. Sliding up her sides, his thumbs just brushing the underside of her breasts and then sliding down onto her lower back, pressing them closer together. Repeat.

Each time she'd wonder if he'd go any further, silently begging him to, but glad he had more self-control than she did since they were in public. His lips on hers became insistent, intense, taking more and more from her, and then he roughly pulled away, pushing her back until there was a huge space between them.

"We better stop."

When she finally found the power of speech she said the most profound thing she could think of. "Mother-of-Pearl!"

Bobby didn't crack a smile. Had she lost her touch that quickly? She hoped not. His shoulders hung low, like he carried the weight of the world on them.

"I need to get back to the bar. Why don't you come with me and I'll get you some coffee?"

"I could use some."

She led the way down the hall. The dinner crowd was brisk and the bar area only had a few open spots. Bobby grabbed the stool at the end like he had the other night with his back to the wall. She went to get the coffee herself, giving her a minute to regroup.

Honestly, she didn't want to regroup. She loved the way he made her feel so out of control. She wanted to tell him to take whatever the hell he wanted from her. To climb the stairs two at a time to her loft and bend her over any piece of furniture they ran into first.

Hot coffee splashed on her hand. She took a few deep breaths, a smile breaking across her face. Wanting a man so bad that her hands shook? That had to be a first for her. She returned to the bar, placing the coffee tray in front of him. He dumped some of the cream in his mug then took a huge gulp.

"You look like you need something stronger than this. Is everything okay?"

Bobby rubbed the back of his neck. "Honestly? No. It's been a hell of day."

She grabbed a beer mug off the drying mat and a towel to wipe it down. "Well, I am the bartender. You want to talk about it?"

"It'll be all around town shortly, so yeah, I would."

"What will?"

"I went to a crime scene this morning at the cemetery."

"At the cemetery? Like grave robbing?"

"No. Theresa Wallace was murdered and dumped there."

"Your stalker?" Drake's words reverberated in her head. *We don't take kindly to those that hurt our kin.* Had his little followers told him that Theresa had been the one that attacked her in front of Bobby's house? Did he retaliate?

"Cassidy? You look white as a sheet."

"Sorry." She blew out a big breath. "That's just awful. I'm sorry you had to see that."

"It was pretty bad. I've seen plenty of dead people, but never a person, you know, that I had dated. Even though she did go a bit crazy, she didn't deserve that."

"You're right. I'm sorry."

The sound of many things breaking had them both looking toward the kitchen.

Bobby set down his coffee mug. "I think a tray of your new dishes just bit the dust."

"I better go see what I need to re-order."

BOBBY DRANK THE REST of his coffee and considered crossing the room to fill his mug again. He'd need more caffeine if he wanted to stay on his feet much longer. A muffled sound from the direction Cassidy had headed had him off his stool and walking her way. Pushing the kitchen door open he immediately ducked when a large carving knife flew toward his head.

Positioning himself behind a wire shelving unit full of dry goods he stuck his head around the corner to see who'd tried to kill him. Two huge, angry looking men were trashing the commercial kitchen. The one closest to him, in a sleeveless T-shirt, threw food from the open refrigerator onto the tiled floor.

The other held Cassidy close, his flannel covered arm around her, his hand over her mouth, while he sent pots, pans, and utensils flying off the counters. Her eyes widened when she spotted him. Anger, like he'd never experienced, bubbled up inside of him against this jackass touching his – touching Cassidy.

"MCPD. Which one of you just threw a knife at my head?"

"Screw you."

Bobby reached for his radio mic then realized he'd taken it off to let it charge in his cruiser. "Now that introductions are over, how about you let the girl go?"

"Screw you."

Another loud crash had Bobby checking around the corner. Sleeveless T-shirt guy had finished in the refrigerator and was now pulling open drawers and dumping their contents. Bobby wondered where all the kitchen staff had gone. He could use another set of hands. And cuffs.

"Hey, fellas. I think that's enough redecorating for the day. How about you both just come over here and put your hands up for me?"

"Screw you."

"That's not annoying at all."

Bobby pulled his firearm and charged around the corner, but the sleeveless guy had moved in on his position, a cast iron skillet already swinging in his direction. Bobby turned, raising his arms to take the hit on his side instead of directly in his face. His body armor vest absorbed most of the blow. Using the man's momentum, Bobby managed to shove the hand with the skillet away from him before raising his weapon to the man's head.

"Stop."

The suspect dropped the pan on the floor causing a deafening clang. The kitchen door swung open and Taylor and Tyler came rushing in.

"What the hell is going on? Get your hands off of her." Taylor O'Hart headed right for the guy holding Cassidy in front of his body like a shield who then pushed her into Taylor's arms.

Bobby pushed sleeveless guy to stand with flannel guy, his gun trained on them both until he could search them for other weapons.

"Both of you turn around and put your hands on top of your head." Relieved seeing Cassidy free from the plaid wearing asshat, Bobby tried to bury his envy at the way she held on to Taylor. "Tyler, you got any cable ties?"

In less than twenty minutes, a squad car pulled out of the Brewhouse parking lot with the two suspects in the back, heading to the MCPD. The twins, Cassidy, and Bobby stood on the sidewalk watching the car drive away.

Bobby faced the two men. "You guys had great timing. Thanks again for the assist."

"I'm just glad one of the crew thought to find us in the back and tell us what was going on," Tyler said.

"I'll need statements from all of you. Let's head back inside."

Taylor, with Cassidy still tucked under his arm, headed toward the door.

She stopped, patting Taylor on the arm as she stepped away from him. "Can you guys just give me a minute with Bobby? We'll be right in."

Although Taylor looked uncomfortable leaving them alone, he and Tyler walked inside. Bobby looked her over. There wasn't a mark on her that he could see, but he could instantly remember that man's hand over her mouth and the look in her eyes.

"You okay? You need something?"

She stepped closer to him. "Yeah, I do need something."

She slid her arms around him, and he gathered her in. A knot of worry inside of him loosened with her head lying against his chest.

"Thank you, Bobby."

"You don't have to thank me for hugs. You can have one any time you want."

She leaned back to look up at him. A smile broke across her face. "I appreciate that, but I meant for what happened in the kitchen."

"What *did* happen in the kitchen?"

"Your guess is as good as mine." She moved out of his arms and started to pace. "When I got in there the dinner crew was gone and those two guys were wrecking everything."

"Any idea who 'those two guys' are?"

"One of the chefs said he recognized them as members of Unite Today."

"Why would they come here?"

She folded her arms across her body. "I have no idea."

"I've got to update my boss, but first I need to take your statements." Bobby struggled with his next words. He didn't want to sound desperate, yet that's exactly how he felt. Desperate to hold her. Kiss her. Have her. "I want you to come to my place tonight. To stay."

"You do?"

"Yes. But, it's up to you. I'll understand if you don't want to. But, you should stay with someone."

"I've got some work to do here, you know, clean-up, repairing our reputation with a few customers that never got their meals. Stuff like that. How 'bout I text you?"

His disappointment nearly made him say something hurtful, but he reined it in. She had every right to push him away knowing his track record. "That's fine. Sure. Let's get these statements done."

CHAPTER TWELVE

Bobby held his front door open and Cassidy stepped past him into the living room. For the first time in hours, she felt grounded again. The encounter with Drake, and then his men, had left her feeling exposed. Being vulnerable sucked and Cassidy wanted to shake it off like a dog shakes off water after a swim. She wanted to be strong and self-sufficient.

Turning toward Bobby, she practically spilled every secret thought and burning wish she had to him on the spot. Had any man ever looked at her like that? With that hunger in his eyes? Truth be told, Bobby scared the hell out of her. Being with him, being without him, they each had their flaws. Yet, life doesn't wait. How much longer would he?

He stood in front of her. Patient. Steady. Powerful. He could be her strength tonight. The temptation of being held won out over her usual stubbornness. She stepped forward and he opened his arms, wrapping them tightly around her. His chest, so warm pressed up against her cheek. So right. She fit perfectly in his arms, his chin brushing the top of her head.

If ever she needed a sign from the universe on whom to trust, it had to be Bobby. He had proved to her he only had her best intentions at heart. But, she knew full well, he only wanted a physical relationship. That had been the plan, and she'd been fine with that. Could she still live with that?

She lifted her head, their gazes meeting. His big brown eyes searched hers. Was he looking for his own sign? Should she say yes to him tonight? Should she end her deliberate suffering and sleep with Bobby Maguire?

"Kiss me. Like you mean it."

He leaned down to capture her lips, kissing her until her toes curled inside her boots. His arms pulled her in closer to his body, his warmth making her yearn to remove his uniform shirt to get closer to all that heat. His lips left hers allowing her some much needed air. She groaned with pleasure as he nibbled on her neck.

"In case you're wondering, I meant every word."

Laughter erupted from her. She loved that he could make her laugh at a time like this. A sharp point of need bloomed inside her and had her making her final decision.

"Bobby. Take me to bed."

His teeth grazed her earlobe, sending bolts of desire through her.

"Are you in full control of all your faculties?"

She pushed him back slightly so she could see his face. "Are you asking if I'm drunk?"

"I am. Asking."

Affecting her practiced southern drawl she said, "I admit I enjoyed some hearty libations at my establishment after this evening's events, kind sir, but I am currently of sound mind and body."

"I'll be happy to verify that for you."

Then she was in his arms, being carried down the hall. No one had ever carried her anywhere. Instead of pleading for him to put her down, she wound her arms around his neck. He walked her into his bedroom, flicking on the light switch as he passed.

The height of his bed had to be four feet off the floor and three times as wide as her own. How many women had he brought in here? She banished the thought. She didn't want to think about that or know the answer.

He placed her on top of the dark comforter, dropped his empty gun belt on a nearby chair, and removed his boots. Stepping closer to the bed he unlaced then pulled her boots off and placed them next to his. He lay down beside her and for a long moment he just looked at her.

Cassidy tugged at the band holding her hair and set it free. "Is anything wrong?"

"Nothing. We waited so long I want to make sure I appreciate every moment."

"It wasn't that long."

"Considering the instant gratification cloud I normally live under, these few weeks have been an eternity." He brushed strands of her hair behind her ear. "But, as it turns out, a welcome change."

"It was hard for me, too, you know. I took a few cold showers."

Bobby's smile warmed the blood in her veins.

"You were thinking about me in the shower?" He scooched closer to her until their bodies touched. He brushed his lips against her cheek, whispering in her ear. "Tell me more about that."

"I think about you all the time."

"Be more specific."

"I specifically think about your mouth." She said, warming up to his request. "How it would feel on my body. I think about your hands, touching me." As she spoke he complied, his lips on her jaw, his hand sliding up her side, moving toward her aching breast. "I think about what it would be like to be taken by you." He gently bit her neck and she sucked in a breath. "Or to take you. To stare into your eyes while I have my way with you."

"God, I love the way you think."

His mouth crushed against hers in a bone melting kiss as his hand finally cupped her breast. His fingers kneaded and heated her flesh through her shirt. He took his sweet time, like he didn't want to miss a thing. Cassidy was no stranger to being swept away during a passionate moment. This couldn't compare to those times. There were no words for how he made her feel. No way to describe how good his hands were on her skin. How his mouth on hers gave as much as it took.

He broke their kiss and rolled to his back to pull off his shirt and she took the opportunity to yank her T-shirt over her head. As she reached for the back clasp on her bra he stopped her.

"You can't wear such sexy underwear and not give me a chance to admire it."

She couldn't argue with him, the bra she had on had been a treat to herself and it was pretty freakin' gorgeous. Black and sheer, low-cut cups, and a little bit of lace. Bobby hungrily gazed at her breasts, her nipples hardening under the sheer material, begging for his touch. He reached behind her to unhook it, sliding the straps down each arm, and then placing it on his nightstand.

"That is a work of art. Never get rid of that," he said before he sucked her nipple into his wet mouth.

Holy crap he was good at that. Her pulse soared when his fingers circled her other nipple. She didn't have the biggest chest, but he didn't seem to mind. His tongue flicked over the bud and she writhed beneath him. She pulled him in closer, his bare skin scorching her as she smoothed her hands over his back and sides, every inch covered in rippling muscle.

His hard length pressed against her leg and she reached for him, cupping him through his pants. He groaned against her breast sending vibrations through her. She knew it would be like this with Bobby. Agonizing pleasure and burning need.

Cassidy pushed on Bobby's chest lightly and he moved back. She pushed again until he rolled to his back. He watched her, his eyebrows scrunched together. When she reached for his belt he slumped back against the pillows and sighed.

"Thought I changed my mind?"

"Actually, yes."

"Not a chance."

He helped her to remove the last of their clothing. Her mouth went dry staring at Bobby in all his glory, all sleek and solid and sexy. She straddled his hips, trapping his hardness beneath her soft folds, slowly moving against him creating the sweetest friction between their bodies.

SOME MIGHT CALL LETTING Cassidy have all the control 'unmanly', but watching her, this magnificent temptress, take what she wanted from him had to be the hottest thing he'd ever witnessed. He wanted to memorize the surreal picture of her over him. The curve of her hips, her long hair brushing lightly, the arch of her back as she moved sensuously against him, her lips parting.

"Cassidy."

"Bobby."

His need to be buried deep inside her grew. "Will you make me beg?"

Her smile was mysterious, like she'd thought about making him beg, but hadn't implemented her plan yet. "Just appreciating the moment."

She moved her hand between them, slipping underneath his length, pressing him more tightly against her wet center. Desire and need consumed him. When her movements faltered, he gripped her hips to continue the sensual slide she'd begun.

Her skin flushed right before she smacked her hand over her mouth to muffle her cry as she climaxed. He groaned as Cassidy rode out her pleasure on top of him. He lifted her, the tip of him brushing her opening, then thrust upwards as he lowered her, her body continuing to shudder as she stretched for him.

"Fuck."

It seemed the only appropriate word to capture his thoughts at that instant. Days and days of imagining what it would be like to have her and not one of his fantasies had come close to the real thing. Before he regained his senses, Cassidy placed her hands on his ribs, lifted herself then glided back down.

"Never stop doing that."

Bobby had to fight for control. She had completely obliterated his self-discipline. Sex had always been good, always been satisfying for him and his partners, but not bone deep staggering. Not brushing up against that door inside him that he kept so tightly closed and locked amazing. How could she make him feel so much?

He pulled her down to his chest then carefully rolled them over. He picked up their pace, wanting to see her drown in pleasure again and desperate to go under with her. Leaning in he kissed her, capturing her tiny moans on his lips.

"Cass."

Her lashes fluttered and she opened her eyes, her gaze locking on to his. Those eyes with their inner light made her appear otherworldly and beautiful. Her arms and legs tightened around him. The skin above her breasts flushed pink and she started to bite down on her lip.

"I want to hear you."

And then she broke apart in his arms, gasping and sighing, her body contracting around him exquisitely. He couldn't look away, their connection being too intense. His final thrusts nearly killed him and then he joined her, his climax tearing through him, before he collapsed on top of her.

He rolled to his side and she stretched out next to him and then flopped an arm and leg over him.

"Woot!"

Cassidy's shout had him laughing out loud. "Woot? That's a first."

"For me, too!"

"Holy crap, Cassidy."

"A-'fucking'-mazing."

He tried to hide his smug smile from her. "I know you're getting comfortable, but I need some water. Do you want me to bring you some, too?"

"Yes, please. I'm parched."

Bobby climbed out of the bed, already missing her limbs tangling with his. He walked the house once more, making sure everything was locked and secured. He filled a glass with water from the pitcher in the fridge, drank it down, then filled it again to bring back to the bedroom. Cassidy had crawled under all the bed covers.

That same warmth he'd only glimpsed the other day at the hospital spread through his chest unchecked. He wanted her there. Out of all the women he'd ever spent time with, she had to be the most unlikely match for him yet she's the one he wanted. He touched her shoulder, but she didn't stir. He put her water on the nightstand then joined her under the covers, pulling her warm body closer.

"I knew it would be good. With you."

He barely made out her mumbled words. She'd been right. Heart-stopping, head-spinning good. Bobby kissed her softly and then nodded off with his face buried in her hair.

CHAPTER THIRTEEN

Cassidy waited for Bobby in his living room. He'd answered the door while talking on the phone, motioned for her to enter, and then disappeared into another room. She wandered the space, screening his media collections on the shelving unit around his TV.

He had varied tastes when it came to books, swinging between fiction and non-fiction. His music was mostly rock and his movies were mostly comedies. At least the music they had in common.

Strong arms wrapped around her from behind, comforting her like a favorite sweater, as Bobby's warm lips touched her check, placing a soft kiss there.

"You feel chilled."

His voice in her ear made her shiver. "It's a little cold in here, but suddenly, I'm warmer."

"Is it a hot flash you're having or maybe a power surge?"

Her elbow found a soft spot in his ribs and he grunted. "That's what you get."

Bobby hugged her in closer. "Have I told you how much I missed you?"

Her breath hitched. She'd bet words like that didn't come easily from him. "You have not."

"Odd."

"You certainly are."

He squeezed her a little tighter until she made a small squeak sound.

"Are you sure you're ready to go to Kate & Rhys's Halloween house warming party? My family is a lot to take all at once."

He'd been warning her about them ever since he asked her to go. She shrugged. "I'm not scared of them."

"They're not scary, but they can get - overwhelming."

"You're overwhelming. All on your own."

"Exactly. I'm just trying to prepare you."

She turned in his arms to face him. No smile, no mischievous glint in his eye. He might be genuinely nervous for her, which would be sweet, but completely unnecessary. "Consider me warned."

She pushed up on her toes to kiss him, softly at first, but touching him brought out an insatiable need in her. She'd left his bed a mere 24 hours ago to go to work and all she wanted, all she'd thought about, was when she could get back to him.

She slid her tongue between his lips to taste him, enjoy him. Hot desire built up inside of her making her want to take all that he could give her and then some. Bobby surprised her when he ended the kiss, leaning his forehead against hers while he regained his breath.

"Keep kissing me like that and we may never get out of here."

"I'm sorry. I don't know what came over me."

He shook his head. "Never be sorry. And, for the record, I really hope that comes over you again later." He reached for her hand, lacing their fingers. Her heart swelled at the gesture. "Come on. The cousins love Halloween so this should be a fun day. Will you be warm enough? I think its outside."

She looked down at her outfit, jeans, a flannel button down, her army jacket and boots. "I should be good."

Riding with Bobby in his muscle car had Cassidy feeling like the prom queen. She turned a bit in her seat so she could watch him drive. He looked relaxed behind the wheel, shedding his serious expression finally for a half smile. She wanted to enjoy the time she had with him while it lasted. Soon, he would realize he'd been with her longer than he wanted, or needed, and she'd be alone again like after her mother passed.

Losing her mom had hurt, but Cassidy had also been thankful. Thankful that her mom didn't have to suffer anymore. Thankful that she'd been with her until the end. Being with Bobby reminded her of what it was like to share a life with someone. Everything about him drew her closer.

Bobby slowed for an intersection with a stop sign. Four men stood next to the sign on the side of the road. Cassidy didn't have to look close to know the men were with the Unite Today membership watch. Bobby stopped his car, but stared straight ahead. He shook his head as he pulled away.

Worse than him dumping her? He'd find out about her relationship to Drake and the Cult and he'd hate her forever. A cold knot of dread settled in her stomach. Either way, she wouldn't have him much longer.

"You want me to turn up the heat?"

"Sorry?"

"You had a little shiver. I thought you might be cold."

"You thought correctly. It must be these awesome leather seats. They're cold on my butt."

"The price we pay for style and comfort."

They pulled up on a sprawling ranch house on a few wooded acres, not nearly as ostentatious as Cassidy thought it would be. Bobby parked his Mustang in the circular driveway at the end of a long line of cars. They walked up the brick stairs together and the door opened before Bobby knocked.

"Last ones to arrive are on dish duty." Kate made a sweeping gesture for them to come inside.

Bobby motioned Cassidy to walk in before him. "There is no way Sam beat me here."

"He did. In fairness, he and Will came over early to work on the haunted cupcake tower."

"Sorry, Cassidy, sounds like we have to wash dishes tonight, although clearly, these people can afford some hired help."

"Why hire when I can get the work done for free? Welcome to our home, Cassidy! What's in the bags?"

"Diet soda." The look on Kate's face had to be a cross between heartbreak and disbelief. Cassidy held the bags toward her. "Kidding. It's beer."

"Thank goodness. Rhys has been looking forward to trying your beer and I didn't know how I was going to break it to him."

"And, you're the first to see the new labels on the bottles created by Bobby Maguire."

"Really?" Kate set down the bags to pull a bottle out. "Bobby! This is beautiful work. I'm so glad you're drawing again. Thank you, Cassidy."

"My pleasure."

"Let's put this in the fridge for safe keeping and then I'll show you guys around."

The house might be unassuming on the outside, but it was beautifully decorated on the inside. Cassidy enjoyed the teasing banter between Bobby and Kate as she led them from room to room of the deceptively large house.

They wound up outside in the expansive backyard where a giant waterfall flowed into the in-ground pool with the hot tub on one end. The majority of people milling about she recognized as Bobby's family and those she didn't know, judging by their size, she guessed were football players.

Huge white tents had been erected in the yard and everywhere she looked movie-style Halloween decorations covered every inch. Purple and orange twinkling lights, giant fuzzy spiders, ghostly sheets, witch hats, skeletons, flying bats, carved pumpkins with flickering candles, black and purple tablecloths.

"There's a fully stocked bar over there, food for weeks on those tables over there, and places to sit around the fire pit there or by the outdoor space heaters under the tent over there." Kate pointed to each area like a flight attendant doing the 'in case of emergency' speech.

Cassidy had never celebrated Halloween. She'd never gone Trick-or-Treating, or worn a costume, or carved a pumpkin and she tried to reign in her inner child as it squealed in delight. "This is amazing."

"This is our favorite holiday. Well, next to Thanksgiving. Hope you're not squeamish because we've got some disgusting fun planned for later."

"That sounds perfect."

Bobby put his hand on her shoulder. "I'm going to grab a beer, Cassidy, you want?"

"Yes, please."

She watched Bobby walk toward the bar in his dark denim jeans and work boots wondering if her nail marks would still be in those ass cheeks.

"I know that look."

"It's a hell of a view." Cassidy turned to face Kate and smiled. "Your home, it's stunning."

Before she could respond a tall handsome man walked over, lifted Kate easily off the ground, and kissed her soundly. He set her back on unsteady feet and Kate swatted at his hands.

"You have to stop doing that in front of guests."

"No, I don't." He grinned at her then turned. "You must be Cassidy. I'm Rhys."

The man towered over her, his hand engulfing hers as he shook it. She looked up at his smiling face and into silver-grey eyes that looked disturbingly like her own. The air in her lungs pushed out all at once and she had to catch her breath before she could respond.

"Yes, that's me. I am."

"I'm glad you could make it. Did you get the 25 cent tour?"

Kate put her hands on her hips. "Is that all you're charging? I've been charging more than that."

Cassidy schooled her features, just barely holding it together, especially since he hadn't seemed to notice anything. "Yes, we did. You have a great place."

"Well, thank you." He pulled Kate closer under his arm. "We were lucky to find it tucked back here in the woods. It's just about everything we were both looking for."

Bobby walked over and handed Cassidy a beer. "Your castle is missing a moat with a drawbridge."

"Bobby! Thanks for coming."

"Wouldn't miss it. It's nice to have you home."

Cassidy appreciated the reprieve as the men shook hands and slapped each other on the backs. What the hell? It was no secret that Drake had fathered other children, besides herself and August, but she hadn't known anything about Rhys. Did he know about them? About her? Did he know who his father was?

"I'm not here long, but we couldn't wait to have everyone over. Dude, come over here. You've got to check out my built-in-grill in the outdoor kitchen."

"Do you even know how to cook?"

As the men walked away talking grilled meats vs. smoked, Cassidy felt Kate's eyes on her. Had the 'town gossip' noticed their matching eye color? Did she see a resemblance, too? What would she say? How could Cassidy explain? She had to throw something out there to prevent crazy questions. "He's bigger than he looks on TV."

Kate bumped their arms together in a friendly gesture. "I think someone's a little star-struck."

Cassidy smiled with relief. "Maybe a little."

"Let's go say hello to Maggie and Emily. We can tell you all about the Decaying Corpse game."

THE TESTOSTERONE BY the grill had to be three men deep. Bobby considered himself a big guy, but compared to some of Rhys's football buddies, he'd still be eating at the kid's table. He pushed his way through the bodies to his family.

"Bobby."

"Chief." He nodded to Jack.

"Bobby."

"Chief." He nodded to Steve.

"Bobby."

"Chef." He nodded to Sam.

"Ha! I like that." Sam bumped his arm against Will "Get it? Chef?"

"I get it." Will rolled his eyes, but bumped Sam back.

Rhys made his way into the circle of men, straightening an imaginary tie. "I'm sure you're all wondering why I called this meeting."

Steve raised his beer bottle. "So we could drink your booze?"

"Precisely. But, you're not getting any of my Cassidy beer."

"Cassidy brought beer?" Jack looked ready to hunt her down.

Rhys held a hand up. "Yes, but I'm saving it. For me."

"She makes some really good beer." Bobby realized how good as he drank from his store bought bottle.

"Speaking of Cassidy," Steve chimed in.

Sam rubbed his hands together. "Here we go."

"What's it been, Bobby? Two full weeks? More?"

"Shut up, Steve."

"Two weeks is like two years in "Bobby Time"," Sam said, using air quotes.

"You can shut up, too."

Steve slapped Bobby on the shoulder. "Have you guys noticed he doesn't use her job description with her name?"

"You mean like Dispatcher Marie, Nurse Kristen, and Teacher Becky?"

Bobby shook his head as Sam ticked off the names on his fingers, thankfully leaving Waitress Theresa off the list.

"Right? It's never Brewmaster Cassidy. Just Cassidy."

"Yeah, yeah, boys, get it all out of your systems."

Rhys tapped him on the arm. "Hey, they have her surrounded."

Bobby looked over his shoulder to see Cassidy in the center of a Maguire woman circle that included his aunts and his mother. She looked like a deer caught in the headlights of an oncoming car.

"What do I do? Should I go over there?"

"Are you crazy?" Jack looked horrified by the thought.

"She's gonna have to hold her own," Sam said.

The whole group of women seemed to hang on Cassidy's every word and then they laughed out loud. The women moved apart and Maggie put her arm through Cassidy's as they walked together to the food tent.

Steve shoved Bobby. "Guess she doesn't need you to rescue her at all."

The men wandered off in separate directions, but Jack stayed, moving closer to Bobby.

"That pair makes me nervous." Jack gestured toward Maggie and Cassidy who were loading plates with cheese and fruit.

"You and me both."

Bobby sipped his beer which had grown warm. He'd honestly prefer to drink Cassidy's beer or nothing at all. It was official, he'd become a beer snob.

"We had an anonymous tip come in at the police station about our case."

"When?"

"About an hour ago. The caller stated there was a car parked in the park & ride that didn't have a permit. The plate comes back to Theresa Wallace's vehicle."

"That's not far from the diner where she worked."

Jack looked around before he continued. "The techs are having it towed to the police station garage before they open it up, but you can see through the window, there's blood on the passenger seat."

"You can? Does that mean you went to see the car?"

"It does."

"You didn't want me to go with you?"

"No need for both of us."

For the first time Bobby had a niggling seed of doubt creep into his mind about Jack's motivations. Did he think he couldn't handle the work after he'd seen Theresa's body? Jack talked about Bobby having trust issues, but he'd never given Jack a reason not trust him. Okay, except for him withholding information about Theresa to begin with.

Bobby put his beer bottle down on a nearby table. "So, we have our crime scene."

"Looks like. They're supposed to call with any other updates."

"You want me to go to the station and supervise?"

"No."

Bobby scrubbed his hand over his face as disbelief and confusion warred inside him. Jack didn't want him to do his job. "Chief, this is important."

"So are days like this. The techs can handle it. Now, let's break those two up over there before they get any weird ideas."

CASSIDY STOOD WITH Bobby on the fringes of a group of Maguires all sitting together by the fire pit watching Kate open a large box. Bobby held her hand against his side while sipping a cup a coffee. He'd been rather distracted since he'd returned from the 'man meets grill' area earlier and he'd never really recovered. She tried not to read anything into that and simply let him be.

Kate's idea of disgusting fun turned out to be putting your hand through holes in cardboard boxes to guess what decaying body parts you were touching. Skinned grapes, wet spaghetti, and a large head of cauliflower could be easily misinterpreted for eyeballs, slimy guts, and a lumpy brain. Cassidy loved every minute and the girls loved having someone new to scare and gross out.

The food had been just as entertaining. The punch bowl was filled with a deep dark red liquid and smoky mist poured over the edges from dry ice. A pumpkin yakking guacamole dip, 'finger' sandwiches, hot dogs wrapped up like mummies, and candy corn gelatin shots were just a few of the dishes.

The haunted cupcake tower had to be four feet tall and built to look like an old castle tower with a spiral ledge from top to bottom. Black and gray icing, dripping blood, and human body parts adorned each cupcake that covered the entire length of ledge. This had to be the best party Cassidy had ever been to.

She could barely keep up with the one-liners and zingers being thrown at each other by family members and yet watching them all joke around made her smile. She thought of her mom a few years after they'd left the compound and how carefree she'd become. No longer worried about something she said or did causing an argument. She hadn't known until then that her mother had a sense of humor.

Out of the box came a large photo album that Kate rested on her lap. As she opened the first page she gasped before she sniffled. It appeared to be full of family photos, some of them from many years ago judging by the black and white prints.

Kate wiped her check on the sleeve of her sweat-jacket. "Rhys, I can't believe you did this."

He stood behind her, his hand on her shoulder. "I had a lot of help from your family. Thank them for getting me all these photos."

"This means so much to me, guys. Thank you."

Bobby leaned over until his lips were close to her ear. "Kate's apartment was over my Aunt's restaurant. When it got torched, she lost everything. Rhys asked for copies of photos we thought she might like to have and he put together the book."

"That's so sweet."

Cassidy had a good feeling about Rhys. She couldn't be happier that he didn't show any signs of being an asshole like Drake and August.

"Aunt Grace! I can't believe you still have this one."

Kate held the book up for them to see a picture of six mostly naked, very dirty children in a small inflatable pool. A tall man in a pair of shorts laughed as he sprayed them with a garden hose. Bobby groaned beside her and she couldn't contain her smirk.

"It's one of my favorites. You kids decided to make mud pies which, of course, turned into a huge mud fight. You were covered from head to toe in dirt and worms. We couldn't let any of you in the house until we got some of the worst off. Robert may have enjoyed spraying you guys down a little too much."

"I think I had mud in my ear for a month after that," Sam said.

"I wonder why 'mud-for-brains' never stuck?" Emily chimed in.

Cassidy squeezed Bobby's hand. "That's your father?"

"Robert Maguire, Sr. He laughed so hard that day. He loved telling that story, too."

"He's so handsome."

"Yeah, he was."

Steve's phone buzzed and after he read the screen he gave a thumbs-up to Kate.

"Thank you, Rhys, for the best present ever." She stood up and kissed him. "But, I may have to top it. Let's go to the driveway!"

Kate's excitement caught on quickly and everyone followed her to the front of the house. A shiny black truck, with a cap, had pulled up near the front door and had the tailgate down. Cassidy had to look over a few heads to finally see there were two pet carriers being pulled out.

"You got me a puppy?"

Rhys sounded like a little kid on Christmas day as Kate handed him a little black lab with a blue bow around his neck and he cuddled it against his chest.

She reached back into the truck and pulled out a golden lab with a pink bow. "I got you two puppies."

"His and Her puppies?"

"If you're going to do it, do it twice," she said.

Cassidy had never heard so much 'ooohing' and 'aaahing' in all her life. She turned to see Bobby's reaction to all the cuteness. Having the full weight of his gaze focused solely on her had the fine hairs on her arms standing up and heat pooling low in her body.

Fierce. Linda had used that word to describe him. Now, Cassidy could feel that intensity all the way down to her toes. He didn't have puppies on his mind at the moment. Without a thought her body turned toward him, like a flower seeking the sun. The corners of his mouth tilted up and he nodded to her.

"Time to go."

CHAPTER FOURTEEN

Bobby pulled into his complex and parked the car. Unhooking his seatbelt, he turned in his seat to face her, so Cassidy unhooked her belt and copied his pose.

"Thank you for coming with me to the party. It was fun."

She tilted her head. "Really? Cause it didn't look to me like you were enjoying yourself that much."

"The beer sucked."

"Does this mean I have successfully converted you?"

"You mean spoiled me? Yes."

"Good. So, the beer stunk, however, the food was amazing. Was it the company?"

"Absolutely not." Bobby sighed. "I can't shut my brain off. That's all."

Cassidy put her hand on his cheek, feeling the lightest bit of stubble on her fingertips. "I might be able to help you with that."

"How so?"

"You know that thing that came over me earlier? Before we left?" Even in the shadowy car, she could see his eyebrows rise up.

"Every momentous second."

"It's about to come over me again."

"Thank the universe."

They met half way, her lips parting under his in a deep, slow kiss. She reached out to pull him in tighter, needing his warmth, except the car didn't have much room for them to maneuver in the leather bucket seats.

She pulled away and fumbled with the door handle. Bobby got out and then he pulled open her door and offered his hand. She gratefully grabbed a hold of it and let him help her from the car. They rushed to his apartment door, his fingers mishandling the keys while he tried to hurriedly unlock it.

The door finally swung open. She walked in ahead of him, removing her coat, and barely catching the hook with it. When the door shut, she spun around to launch into his arms and Bobby caught her easily. He kissed her hungrily as he tucked her in snugly against him. How had she made it through the whole day without his lips on hers?

He pressed her body up against the nearest wall. He lowered her feet to the floor, his fingers in her hair turning her head, kissing her longer and deeper. She didn't know if his brain had shut off, but hers certainly had. He eased back enough to look at her, his eyes all but scorching her with their bronze piercing stare.

"Cass, I need you."

He sounded as desperate for her as she craved him. "Then have me."

HER WORDS SET A FIRE inside him, cranking his desire up another notch. He lowered his mouth to hers again, his tongue sliding along her lips before plunging between them. She wrapped her arms around his shoulders, pressing her breasts against his chest. At this rate, he'd never make the bedroom.

Bobby grabbed under her ass, picking her back up and walking further into the living room. He sat in the middle of his couch, Cassidy's knees sliding down on either side of his thighs, straddling him.

"I've thought about you and this body all day today." Bobby unbuttoned her flannel then pushed it off her shoulders. "How much I wanted to see it naked was high on the list, but I just want to feel you against me. The softness of your skin haunts me."

Once he had her shirt off, he slid his hands up her arms and shoulders, down over her breasts and onto her stomach.

"You're so goddamn pretty." He put his lips on her skin and then licked up toward her breasts. "I would just picture your body and get hard for you."

His words were having the desired effect as Cassidy moved against him and fine beads of sweat broke out across her skin. His fingers opened her bra and he grasped both breasts, using his thumbs on her nipples making her moan and shiver.

"That's the exact sound I remember. Dammit, woman. What are you doing to me?"

He worshipped her breasts with his hands and mouth until her words became incoherent. His hands shook as he worked on the clasp to her pants. This must be what junkies feel when they need their fix.

He'd never craved a woman so badly. Why her, he had no idea, but he had to be inside her, he had to claim her. His movements were clumsy, but he managed to get them mostly undressed and her lying on the couch beneath him. As a teen he hadn't been this anxious.

"Jesus, you've got me shaking."

She shifted underneath him. "I'll beg if I have to."

Her smile had sassy written all over it as she reminded him he'd said something similar to her. There may be days he would tease her, days he would make her beg. But, not today.

"That won't be necessary."

With one hard thrust, he pushed himself into her, her nails sinking into the muscles of his back. The sting helped distract him from how amazing she felt closing around him. Pulling back, he rocked into her again, his whole body aching for more.

"Faster."

"No way I'm rushing this."

He controlled their pace with slow and powerful strokes, building their desire, carrying them to greater heights.

Football stats. Bullet calibers. He had to focus on something or it would be all over too soon. Her body tightened more, wonderfully, around him. That didn't help. How could he ever give this up? He had an addiction. To her. And he didn't think he could break it, or if he wanted to.

"Bobby."

His name on her lips, like a plea, spurred him on. No more holding back. He drove harder into her again and again, her body bowing beneath his bringing her breasts closer. He pulled her nipple into his mouth and swirled his tongue around the center.

"Yes!"

Her hands grabbed his head, holding him in place, as she found her release. He sucked harder as he plunged into her over and over, trying to prolong her pleasure, until he couldn't hold back. He let go, falling over the edge with her, a strangled groan escaping him as he reached a new high. Contentment washed over him as he gathered her closer, where she belonged.

CHAPTER FIFTEEN

The ringing wouldn't stop. Cassidy opened her eyes to a dark room and a warm body next to her. Bobby. She lay curled up behind him in his bed, wearing only his T-shirt she'd put on in the middle of the night. This might be the best wake up she'd ever had, except for the phone that kept ringing. When a second phone rang, Bobby groaned next to her, then sat up and reached for his mobile.

"Maguire."

Cassidy slipped out the other side of the bed to check in the living room for the remainder of her clothes. She picked up their things from the floor, smiling at the memory of their wild and unstoppable passion that caused their garments to be strewn all over and her bra to be shoved between the couch cushions. Her arms loaded, she reached the bedroom doorway when Bobby stood, clutching the sheet around his lower body.

"That's not possible."

Bobby's eyes were wide open, looking her way, but not at her.

"Why can't I just come in to the station? Fine. I'll wait for them here."

He hung up the phone and tossed it on the bed. He grabbed the back of his neck then snapped his head to the right and left, the cracking noises echoed in the room.

"Please don't take this the wrong way, Cassidy, but you've got to get dressed and get the hell out of here."

"What happened?"

"That was Jack. An anonymous tip led to Theresa Wallace's car yesterday and the techs found the murder weapon on the floor. It's a tactical knife. All the MCPD cops have one. This one has my initials on it."

"What?"

"There's some other circumstantial evidence pointing my way and protocol states that Jack had to contact the county sheriffs in Mount Eve to assist with the investigation. They're coming here to take me in for questioning. I don't want you here, when they get here."

His voice sounded colder than the walk-in freezer at the brewery. She didn't need to be told twice. She ducked into the bathroom to dress. When she came out, Bobby had donned his uniform, complete with a black baseball hat pulled low over his eyes.

Everything inside her wanted to reach for him, to comfort him, to tell him that it would be all right. He walked out of the bedroom before she could say a word. She followed him out, all the way to the front door.

Her stomach clenched. Any words she might want to say were getting stuck in her throat. He took her jacket off the hook and as he handed it to her a knock sounded.

"Shit."

"Listen, Bobby, don't be naïve, okay? Get yourself a lawyer or a representative. Someone to look after you."

He stared at her, the crease in his forehead made her think she'd spoken another language.

"Don't be your regular sarcastic self, either. Cops don't think that's funny. Be direct and don't get emotional."

"Why are you telling me this?"

She pulled her jacket on. "Because the system doesn't always work for innocent people. You can get railroaded if they don't have anyone else to question."

He shook his head. "Innocent? Are you sure about that?"

"Yes, I am. You'd never harm Theresa. No matter what she did."

His shoulders slumped. "I'm sorry, Cass. There was supposed to be coffee and pancakes this morning and instead…"

"Hey, I'm a big girl. I get it."

"I don't. I don't understand what the hell is going on."

She put her hand on his arm. "You've got to wake up, Bobby. You didn't do this, but someone's making it look like you did. You need to protect yourself."

He nodded, then took a deep breath, when another knock sounded at the door.

"I want you to leave before I do."

He kissed her cheek, then he opened the door where two officers stood on his front step.

"Neil. Marc."

"Bobby." The taller one greeted him and then they all shook hands as if this were a polite visit. "We request your cooperation in our investigation. We'd like you to come to the Sheriff's Office with us."

"Thank you. If you would allow my guest to leave, I'll be happy to cooperate."

They moved to the side and let Cassidy walk by. She stood by her car in the lot watching them escort Bobby to their vehicle. They stood near the back door talking for a moment before Bobby handed his holstered weapon over to one of them. Cassidy's stomach turned queasy. She should've told Bobby about Drake. She should've shared her suspicions. Because watching a police car drive away with the only person she cared about in the world, might be more than she could handle.

IT IMPRESSED BOBBY that the sheriffs had managed to find one of the few deputies he didn't know to question him for four hours straight. Nerves were getting the better of the new guy and he'd blown right through his deodorant, stinking up the room.

The pile of evidence illustrating Theresa's relentless stalking of Bobby, which Jack had to turn over, kept coming up again and again as motive for her murder. They assumed that Bobby would kill her because she kept leaving him bloody dolls at his doorstep. That he would slice her throat because she'd attacked his 'friend' with a beer bottle.

He stayed as calm as he could during all the accusations and lies hurled his way. He knew the drill. He also knew Jack wasn't far away, working his ass off trying to find the truth. Mostly he knew his own innocence would clear his name.

The door opened and Bobby mentally crossed his fingers that they were about to release him, but the look on Jack's face wiped his hope away. In a haze, Bobby listened as Jack told him about the murder weapon. That it had Bobby's prints all over it. That it had blood on it that matched Theresa's type. That DNA tests were being run.

That evidence had been found at Theresa's apartment that Bobby had been there. That he'd confronted Theresa with evidence of her stalking. That there appeared to be a struggle. That the ADA had read Bobby's notes and reports about the stalking. That the ADA, afraid their office might be accused of favoritism, decided there was enough evidence to arrest Bobby for Theresa's murder.

Sick. Bobby's gut burned empty. Like it had been scooped out and left hollow. He understood why Jack chose to put the handcuffs on him himself, to spare him the embarrassment of anyone else doing it, yet it had to be the worst moment of his life. Well, on top of being accused of murder. And having to turn over his badge and gun. And being read his rights.

This couldn't be happening. It had to be a nightmare. Jack assured him that he knew Bobby was innocent. That he'd find out what really happened. It didn't make it any easier. Any less painful. Any less real. He'd lived a lot of things down in his hometown, but nothing like this.

He wondered if handcuffs felt different on an innocent man. Did the guilty feel like this? Betrayed? Trapped? Ready to chew their own arm off.? It had to be enough to know the guys had his back. That the charges were completely bogus and he would get his day in court and the truth will prevail. Right?

"Bobby. It's time to go."

Jack's voice, laced with regret, penetrated the fog around Bobby's head. He nodded to his friend and they walked out of the interrogation room together, but the Sheriffs wouldn't allow Jack to stay while they booked him. Truthfully, Bobby didn't want anyone to see him pose for his mugshot. This just couldn't be happening.

CHAPTER SIXTEEN

The stainless steel fermentation tank wouldn't get any shinier and Cassidy knew it, yet she continued to scrub at it like she could change the outcome. She'd hoped the hard, sweaty work would help keep Bobby off her mind. Hours had passed and she still hadn't heard from him. At this point she didn't know if she would. He had no reason to call her.

She couldn't figure out a way to help him either, she had no real proof of wrongdoing, but it didn't lessen her feeling of responsibility. And guilt. Bobby would never hurt anyone, not even Theresa, so this had to be a setup. And, after hearing how Drake felt about Bobby shooting his dim-witted son, who else would set him up for a crime he didn't commit other than Drake? She should've told Bobby. She should've told him about Drake and what he'd said to her that day behind the Brewhouse.

"Cassidy Valentine Drake?"

Cassidy whipped around to find Jack Munro standing a few feet behind her dressed in his MCPD finest.

"You're pretty ninja-like considering how much hardware you carry on your superhero belt."

"It's a gift."

Cassidy let out a long breath, then walked toward the sink with the tank cleaner bottle and rag to put them away and wash her hands. "You must have run my fingerprints to come up with my birth name."

"I did. Got 'em off of one of your beer bottles. Truly some of the best beer I've ever had, by the way."

"I'm glad you enjoyed it. What made you even check them?"

"When I saw you standing with Rhys MacGrath at the party I noticed the resemblance and the similarity of your eye color." He walked closer and leaned on the wall near her. "I happen to know he inherited that particular shade from his biological father."

Shame filled her. If Jack knew about her father, it wouldn't be long before everyone knew. She dried her hands with a paper towel, then turned to face him. "I suppose you saw the reason my prints were in the system?"

"I did. At age eleven you broke into a sporting goods store two towns over. You were arrested before you could remove anything, so you were charged with trespassing. Your record was not sealed."

"Drake didn't bother to pay for lawyers. If you got caught you were on your own."

Jack scratched his chin. "What were you supposed to steal that day?"

"Ammo. As much as I could carry."

"Drake never sent you out again."

"Guess you would ace that detective's exam, huh?" She shook her head. "No. He never trusted me after that. Said the only way the cops would've known I was there was if I called them."

"Did you?"

"I did." Cassidy tried to shake off her unease. She'd never told anyone half of what she'd just confessed to Jack. It had to be those ice blue eyes.

"Did you know you were related to Rhys?"

She released another long breath. "Not until I met him."

"And you always knew Drake was your father?"

"Unfortunately."

"Why don't you give me the short version?"

"Why don't you tell me about Bobby first?"

He crossed his arms over his chest. "Bobby's in trouble. While he was being questioned by the sheriffs some test results came back on the murder weapon. They found traces of blood on the knife and it's the same type as Theresa's. They're running DNA. It could take a while."

"What about an alibi?"

"We're trying to establish a timeline from when Theresa left work until her body was discovered. None of this stuff happens as fast as it does on TV."

"You know Bobby's innocent."

"I do. I want to know who set him up and how. Now, it's your turn."

How much should she tell him? Nothing? Everything? Did she have a choice? He already knew her name, she should just fill in the blanks for him or he would do it himself.

"Short version? I was born at the Unite Today compound. When I was 13 my mother, Ruby, packed a bag for each of us and we left in the middle of the night."

"You lost your mom recently?"

She leaned her hip on the counter next to her, letting it bear her weight. "Yes, to cancer."

"I'm sorry, Cassidy."

"Thank you."

"What I can't figure out is how the Maguire women don't know about you and the Cult. How is it possible to keep a secret that big from them?"

"I've never told anyone and no one ever asked. My mom had my name legally changed to her last name, Conklin."

"How much of this does Bobby know?"

"None." Jack's eyes bore a hole straight through her. "I don't normally lead with that info. Nice to see you, have a beer, my dad's the leader of a cult. Besides, I'm sure he's going to punch out soon anyway. Why make things messy?"

"Punch out? You think Bobby's done dating you?"

"Sure. He's sweet an' all, but we all know he doesn't do relationships."

"I know that's been the way with Bobby, for most of his life, but I'm not sure that's what's going on here."

She shook her head. "It doesn't matter. So, what is it that you think I can tell you?"

From his jacket pocket he removed a small pad of paper and a pen. "I want to know about Drake's operations at the compound."

"I haven't lived there in years. I can't help you with that."

Jack pushed off the wall, taking a step closer. "I just put handcuffs on my best friend. I had to take his gun and badge. So, what I'd like to hear from you is absolutely any and all information that you can share about the compound. Old or new. Relevant or not. I'm going after Drake for framing Bobby so I need details, I need names, I need everything you got. And, understand that my objective is to end Drake's operations here in Maguire's Corner. For good."

His intensity made sense after all that Drake had done to this town. She had to admit, Police Chief Jack Munro intimidated the hell out of her. "There are women and children up there, too. Innocent women and children."

"I'm aware of that."

And he would be. She'd bet he'd do his due diligence before he ever made a move. Those families would be safe. Cassidy crossed her arms. It was time for her to stop feeling guilty. Maybe this would be the way she could help Bobby.

"The men at the compound are well armed, they're well trained, and they're very dangerous. They sell drugs to finance their operations and steal to cover the rest. Since it gets pretty boring up there, most of them are addicted to drugs and alcohol. Drake is committed and fanatical about whatever he deems important to him at that moment. And, he's unstable. He's got a thing for washing down pain pills with booze and screwing the widowed moms."

"I need to know more."

"You're going to need more paper."

BOBBY HAD NEVER BEEN to the holding cell area of the jail before. It wasn't a pleasant experience. John, another deputy he knew, walked him down a long corridor. Instead of bars, the cells had actual doors with a small window and they were all occupied. He'd be locked in his own eight by eight soon enough. His stomach clenched.

How had his knife shown up at the crime scene? When had he last seen that knife? At work? At home? They stopped in front of an open door. Without being told, Bobby walked in. It took all of two seconds to see the whole cell. Metal slab hanging against the back wall that functioned as a seat or a bed, metal desk on the right, next to a metal toilet. Between the crappy yellowish lighting and the rough concrete floors, his optimism slipped further away.

"Sorry, Bobby."

"Hey, I get it. You're just doing your job."

"I'll see if I can bring you some coffee in a bit."

"Thanks."

The door closed and locked tight with a snap. Bobby sank down on the bench, resting his spinning head in his hands, while he tried to come up with answers to so many questions. There had to be an explanation. For all of it. Especially his knife.

Round and round his thoughts went and each time it all came back to Theresa. It had to be her. She must have taken the knife from his house. From his garage. And then she told someone. That man. The one he'd heard in the background of their phone conversation at the police station, the one she'd called her 'new friend'. She must have told that man she had Bobby's knife and then he used it to kill her. Why? Because he works for Drake.

Bobby stood and reached for his phone then remembered he'd handed it in to the property guy with all his other personal items when he'd been booked. This sucked. He needed Jack to find out where she'd placed that call from. He paced the small cell while another piece of the puzzle occurred to him. The anonymous tip that led to Theresa's car and the murder weapon had to be the same man that killed her.

He took a deep breath and let it out slowly. He'd have to be patient. He'd get a message to Jack when John came back. Meanwhile, he knew Jack would figure out Theresa's time of death which would lead them to the conclusion that Bobby couldn't have killed her.

A noise outside his cell had him breaking out in a cold sweat. He moved back, as far as he could, as a deputy he didn't recognize swung open his door. Standing with him were two guys in orange jumpsuits. Bobby recognized them as the same two that had wrecked the Brewhouse kitchen.

"Brought you some visitors, Maguire. Compliments of August Drake. He's just a few doors down."

"It's not even my birthday."

"Oh, it's not a gift."

"Well, at least tell me your name so I can send a thank you note."

"Baker. I'll leave you to get reacquainted with Jed and Lance."

Baker ushered the men inside and closed the door leaving the already small cell incredibly crowded. One of the men cracked his knuckles while the other rolled up his jumpsuit sleeves. Bobby knew he had one chance to get the upper hand.

"Jed?"

The knuckle-cracker looked over at his friend revealing their identities. Now Bobby knew the one named Jed was the one that had put his hands on Cassidy.

"Sorry, Lance."

Pushing hard off the wall Bobby kicked Lance directly in the kneecap, the solid rubber sole of his boot making contact with a satisfying crunch. Lance crumpled to the ground, his scream echoing in the small room. Bobby stepped over him toward the right hand side of the cell.

"You sure you want to do this, Jed?"

"Screw you."

"Again, with the stunning commentary."

Jed kept looking from his friend on the floor, to Bobby, and back to his friend. Bobby could wait him out, but he didn't want Lance to make a quick recovery and make it two against one again. He took one step forward and Jed jumped him. They stumbled back to the bench with Jed trying to bash Bobby's head against the wall.

Jack would be proud that Bobby's close combat training kicked in. He hooked a foot behind Jed's leg and shoved him to the side. Following the man's movement, Bobby punched him in the jaw. The hit didn't have the desired effect and Jed swung right back, glancing Bobby's chin.

Bobby advanced, pushing both hands into Jed's chest, shoving him down on the bench. He followed it up with another punch straight down to the side of his face. The man's head must be made of cement and the hit reverberated all the way up Bobby's arm into his shoulder.

The cell door open behind him and Bobby quickly turned, putting his hands up. Baker walked toward him, holding a night stick, and he swung it like a bat, striking him in the side.

"Up against the wall, Maguire!"

Bobby gritted his teeth while the pain rushed through him like the tide coming in. He wanted to argue, but it would be his word against the deputy, so he turned to face the wall. Baker struck him in the side again.

A hand grabbed the back of Bobby's shirt pulling him around so he faced Jed who reached back and swung his beefy fist into the side of his face. Bobby tasted blood and his head buzzed. He braced for the next hit as Baker's night stick found his side again, pushing the air from his lungs.

"What the hell is going on in here?" John stood outside the doorway.

Baker smacked the night stick against his palm. "I got this, John. You don't need to be here."

"You two, back away from Maguire. Now."

"I said, I got this."

John rested his hand on his firearm. "Back. Up. Now."

Baker and Jed moved away from Bobby, stepping over Lance, who still lay on the floor holding his knee.

"You okay, Maguire?"

With super-human willpower, Bobby managed to push off from the wall and move his sore body toward the door without grabbing his aching side. "I am now. Thank you."

John moved back so Bobby could move outside the cell. "I was coming to tell you that you're being released. The timeline didn't work out and you have a rock solid alibi for when the girl was murdered."

"That's the news I've been waiting for."

"Tell me what happened in here before you go."

Bobby looked at the men, pleased he wouldn't be the only one nursing bruises. "This? Just a couple of schoolyard bullies."

Baker spit on the floor. "Watch your back, Maguire."

John pointed out the door. "Head to the left and look for Neil. I'll take care of these guys."

THE RELEASE PROCESS didn't take long and in less than thirty minutes Bobby left the sheriff's office a free man, with their sincere apologies. He stood on the sidewalk without a ride, no badge or gun, bruised ribs, a dead mobile phone, and in desperate need of coffee. He needed to talk to Jack, but it'd be a cold day in hell before he'd go back into the sheriff's office to make that call.

A gas station stood on the next block over. He headed in that direction hoping they still had a pay phone. He wanted to get home and have a nice hot shower. And coffee. And something to eat. And, he wanted to talk to Cassidy. She must be wondering what had happened to him after he'd been taken away this morning. If that alone hadn't screwed everything up for them.

Tires screeched next to him and Bobby turned to see the Unite Today van come to a stop at the curb. The side door slid open and two men jumped out. They grabbed his arms pulling him toward the vehicle.

Bobby's surprise turned quickly to alarm at the strength and intent of the men. Adrenaline kicked in, and he had almost broken free from their grasp, when the sound of a gun racking caught his attention. The driver pointed the barrel directly at him from inside the van.

"Mr. Drake would like to see you."

"Tell him to make an appointment during office hours."

"He would prefer to meet in private."

Bobby tried to pull away from the men again, but they had a tight hold on him. "Look, I'm sure you're an awesome henchman, but I'm not going with you."

"He didn't specify how I delivered you."

Bobby's choices were extremely limited. Not only was he exhausted, but firearms beat bare fists every day. This guy might shoot him just for the fun of it.

"Fine, but don't expect a good review on your social media page."

He climbed into the middle seat of the van and the two men sat on the bench seat behind him. The trip wasn't long and Bobby recognized where they were immediately, the house where the MCPD had had their evening drug raid on August and his buddies.

Everyone piled out of the van, but only the driver walked Bobby through front door. One small gas lantern set on a card table lit the area that used to be the living room of this house. Next to the cold fireplace stood none other than Drake.

Bobby hadn't seen him in person in years and although he had aged, he still carried an air of authority about him. Drake's size and stature were clearly something Rhys had inherited from him, as well as the odd eye color.

"Drake. Nice place you've got here."

"Maguire. I assume I have you to thank for cutting all the utilities to the house?"

"You can send a donation to the PBA."

"Always the witty one."

"You flatter me."

Drake moved closer to the table. "Big day for you, getting out of jail."

"It is. I was just headed home to celebrate."

"I'm sure you had one of your corrupt police friends lie and give you an alibi?"

"I didn't have to. I was working the night you had Theresa murdered."

"You could have killed her while on duty."

"I suppose that would be an option, but about thirty witnesses put me at the scene of a two car motor vehicle accident. For hours. Your spies must have missed that little fact."

Drake kicked a piece of a broken brick by his foot. "It wouldn't matter. You Maguires always manage to worm your way out of trouble and responsibility."

"You mean like you do Drake? Cause you're so innocent? Like August is innocent? He was selling heroin out of this very house. Don't you care that your drugs are killing kids in this town?"

"That's your problem, not mine."

"You just create the problem and we have to clean it up? Just pass the buck, right? Not the tallest tree in the forest, are you?"

"You watch your mouth."

"Is this your big plan? You drag me out here for payback and then head back to the compound like none of it ever happened?"

"You may think I'm stupid, Maguire, but I'm not telling you anything. I brought you here to even the score for what you did to August. Eye for an eye. That sort of thing. You don't need to know anything else."

The front door opened and two large men strode in, pulling a hooded figure with them.

Drake approached the newcomers "What is this? You're supposed to be at the compound."

Anger ripped through Bobby as they pulled off the hood and he recognized the purple streaked black hair girl beneath. Cassidy blinked her eyes rapidly. She looked unharmed, except for the tight plastic ties around her wrists.

"What are you doing bringing her here?"

Shit! Bobby automatically took a step toward Cassidy and had to stop himself. That stupid watch group must have seen her with him. They must have assumed grabbing her would compromise him somehow. If they hurt her, there'd be no one to blame but him.

"This one showed up at the compound asking for you. Said she had to talk to you real bad. Claims she's your daughter."

CHAPTER SEVENTEEN

Cassidy's heart beat frantically in her chest. She'd had no idea where the men were taking her or what they would do when they got there. She kept blinking to get her eyes to adjust to the dim light after the dark bag had been over her head for so long. Looking to her right she caught sight of Bobby.

"She is my daughter. Why would you bring her here?"

Her surprise and relief turned to dread. Cassidy remembered why she didn't tell people that personal fact upon seeing the mix of confusion and disgust cross Bobby's face. Like hearing the words made him physically ill.

"You said if anything strange happened you wanted to know about it right away."

"I meant call me, not kidnap anyone."

Cassidy stepped closer to Drake. "What the hell is going on here?"

Drake grabbed her arm roughly. "Why did you go to the compound, Cassidy? Have you come to your senses? Were you returning home?"

"Of course not. I wanted to talk you out of doing anything else crazy, but I guess that's too much to ask at this point. Let Bobby go. You've done enough. Leave him alone."

She couldn't look at Bobby again. She couldn't bear to see the look on his face now. All her secrets had been revealed. She never wanted him to find out this way.

"Enough? I've done enough? No! You haven't seen anything yet. William, you keep an eye on her. You two, help me with Maguire."

William yanked Cassidy against his side. When she tried to pull away he removed a gun from his pocket and shoved it into her ribs.

Helplessly she watched as the men pressed down on Bobby shoulders, forcing him to his knees.

Drake chose a broken brick from the floor near the fireplace then walked back to tower over Bobby. "First, I cast doubt about you. Then I took your badge. Then, your freedom. I'm going to take this whole damn town from you, too. Before I do, I'll take the very thing that caused my son's dishonor."

"August didn't need any help dishonoring himself."

"Hold him!" Drake slammed his hand on the table. "I want his right hand, right here!"

The men struggled to pin Bobby down and pull his right arm across the table. Bobby appeared to go limp and then he slammed his elbow back into the groin of the man next to him. The man fell back, clutching his crotch.

Cassidy needed to do something. She couldn't let this happen. She tried again to pull away from the man holding her, but he jammed the gun harder into her side. "Drake, stop! He's a police officer."

Drake shouted for the others to come from outside to help. Now there were three men holding Bobby while the fourth one rolled around on the floor holding himself and whimpering.

"Don't do this." Warm tears slipped down Cassidy's cheeks. "Don't hurt him."

Drake loomed over Bobby. "It's done. Look what happened to you since you've been with him! He put you in harm's way, he crippled my son, and now I will do the same to him." He leaned down to look Bobby in the eyes. "You will never harm my family again."

The horror of watching one man torture another would always stay with Cassidy. She begged Drake to stop each time he lifted the brick. Bobby never let up trying to pull his arm back, trying to free himself until he passed out, his cheek hitting the edge of the table before the dead weight of his body pulled the men off balance and they let him slide to the floor.

THE NIGHTMARE WAS REAL. Bursts of fiery pain battered against him as Bobby woke, lying on the floor of the former drug house, his throbbing hand crushed and bloody. Waves of nausea threatened to overtake him as he managed to slowly sit up.

"Everyone is outside. I'm almost out of these ties. Then I can help you."

Cassidy. She sat on the floor a few feet away. What did it mean that the sound of her voice settled him and yet infuriated him at the same time? He couldn't be any angrier with her. It boiled inside him. How could she just sit there like she hadn't completely betrayed his trust?

Vision wavering, he had trouble seeing just what her cable tied hands were doing besides fussing with the laces on her boots. So many heated words sprang to his mind, but he kept them to himself. Getting them both out of here alive would have to top the priority list.

"You should have told me. About everything."

Damn. He hadn't meant to say that. At least not out loud. Cassidy stopped her movements and looked at him. Her make-up had smudged under her eyes and her lip was split and swelling. Her eyes. Her silver-gray otherworldly eyes. The ones that looked just like Drake's. How had he never put that together before?

"I don't remember you telling me every gory detail of your childhood either."

"Some details are gorier than others." Damn. He didn't mean to say that either. "Who hit you?"

"They might all come strolling back in here at any second. Let's not lose sight of the objective."

"How long have they been outside?"

She turned back to her boots. "Maybe five minutes."

"What about your phone?"

"They have it."

Another wave of pain hit and he had to take a few breaths to get through it. "What are you doing with your feet?"

Cassidy lifted her legs showing him that she'd tied her boot laces around the cable tie. She moved her feet back and forth a few times, like she was riding an invisible bike, and the plastic snapped. She untied the laces, then crawled across the floor toward him. Reaching his side, she removed her flannel shirt, leaving her in just a black tank top.

"I need to wrap this up. This is going to hurt."

With a little effort, and lots of splintering pain, she made her shirt a sling for him, tying the sleeves around his neck, to support his damaged hand.

"Holy shit." He cursed some more under his breath. "Thank you, I think. Can you help me up?"

Once standing Bobby wanted to yack all over the floor. His head might actually be splitting open and he had to breathe through the pain to keep from spilling his guts.

"If you're wondering why your head hurts, you hit your face on the table and your head on the floor when they dropped you. I wouldn't be surprised if you have a concussion."

"I'll have to worry about that later. Okay, we have to get to the sliding glass doors on the side of the house. It's a straight shot to the woods from there."

She walked ahead of him, quietly moving things that might get into his way. When they reached the dirty glass doors they slipped outside and he motioned for them to stop. He welcomed the cold, fresh air into his lungs. The sun had mostly set and brilliant orange and red colors filled the sky. Bobby checked the area around them thoroughly and didn't catch sight of anyone on this side of the house.

"Once we start, don't stop running. It's just a couple of miles through the woods and we'll be pretty close to the firehouse. Ready?"

"Right behind you."

They headed quickly in the direction of the trees, each step jarring his hand until he wanted to scream, but he sighed with relief when they reached the tree line and they could rest for a moment.

"I hear voices," Cassidy said from his right.

He could hear them, too. No rest for the weary. "They're catching up. Let's move."

They headed into the trees. A man shouted to 'fan out' and it pushed him faster through the low branches. Bobby wanted to run in a straight line, but the terrain became impassable and he had to zig zag around in the woods. He could no longer tell if they would come out in the right area.

What little light the sunset had provided earlier, faded, and it became more difficult to distinguish the landscape. Cassidy kept up with him, never uttering a complaint, though she had to be freezing and probably scared. He wanted to ask how she was doing, but his pride kept him from conversing with her. He had a lot of important questions to ask her, especially about Drake, but this wasn't the time or place.

Pain rolled through him each time his hand jostled against his body and his head screamed like it might explode, but he kept moving, knowing they had no other choice. The footsteps behind them faded and Bobby found his second wind. Pushing through some bushes he stood on the edge of an open field. He knew exactly where they were now.

A gunshot rang out and a split-second later the tree branch next to his head splintered from the impact.

"Down."

They ducked behind the tree just as another shot rang out, the bullet whizzing past them. They had maybe another fifty yards to go before they'd reach the firehouse. If he had any luck left there'd be someone there to help. Taking a few deep breaths he psyched himself up to make the final dash.

"This is it. Across the field, toward the right. Don't stop."

A third gunshot convinced him they needed to get moving. They made a break for it and Bobby ran as fast as he could, Cassidy right on his heels. Blood pounded in his ears from his efforts to get through the tall grass. A few more shots rang out behind them and then finally the rear of the firehouse came into view. They rounded the corner and ran right into Steve.

"What the fu...Bobby! Where did you come from?"

"We need to get inside."

"Were those gunshots?"

"Inside. Now!"

Steve used his keycard to open the door for them and they entered the building.

"Call Jack and tell him to bring back up."

"I'm on it."

Bobby fell into the nearest chair, pain and exhaustion swamping him. He vaguely listened to Steve on the phone. Cassidy stood near the roll up bay doors looking out the small window.

Bobby's eyes snapped open. "Can they get in any other door?"

"No, we're locked up tight here. Who's shooting at you?"

"Drake's men."

Cassidy leaned back against the door. "I hear sirens."

"Hopefully that will scare off whoever is out there."

A few minutes later, Steve opened the door for Jack, and some of his officers. Jack headed straight to Bobby.

"You never write, you never call. You know how much that annoys your sister."

"Nice to see you too, Jack."

"Fill me in."

Bobby gave him a quick and dirty rundown of what had happened in the last few hours. Surprisingly, Jack didn't ask him a million questions. It could be because he was barely staying conscious while he shared his story. When he got to the part about Cassidy, he glossed over any mention of her relationship to Drake. Not his secret to share.

Pointing at two officers, Jack said, "Get a few more guys, Sean and his K-9. I want you to sweep the property between here and that house. I'm sure they've all scattered, but we need to check. I'll take Bobby to the hospital myself."

Steve helped Bobby up from the chair. "I'll go too, Jack."

Bobby used his good arm to stop Steve from moving him. "What about Cass?"

They turned as a unit to look at her and the sight in front of Bobby might haunt him for the rest of his life. Bright red blood smeared down the door to where Cassidy now sat on the floor. Her two hands pressed against her left side, blood seeping between her fingers.

CHAPTER EIGHTEEN

"Cassidy!"

She lifted her head and her eyes rolled back. Steve let go of him so quick that Bobby fell back into the chair. His cousin pulled a red medical bag out of a compartment on the back of the fire engine and fell to his knees next to Cassidy, whose skin had turned pale and waxy. He unzipped the bag and pulled out flat white packages.

"Jack, help me open these gauze pads, then go pull your truck up to the door. We've got to get her to the hospital."

"I can call the ambulance."

"It'll take too long to crew. We'll take her."

The pads started to pile up on her thigh and then Steve picked them all up and stuffed them into her bleeding side. Her groan of pain echoed in the firehouse.

"That got her attention." Her body shook making the metal door rattle behind her. "She's going into shock. Go Jack. I'll meet you at the door with her."

"Bobby. You come with me."

Numbly, Bobby followed Jack to his truck and climbed into the back seat while his mind raced. Cassidy's been shot. Cassidy's bleeding out because she's been shot. She'd been running behind him, protecting him. She'd taken a bullet for him.

Jack pulled up to the door where Steve held Cassidy in his arms. The two men were able to lay her on the back seat, her head on Bobby's lap.

Steve grabbed Bobby's good hand and pressed it down hard on her bleeding side. "Keep pressure here." He slammed the truck door and hopped into the front with Jack and they took off.

"Hold on, Cassidy. We're going to the hospital."

Bobby had to lean down to hear her response over the loud siren from Jack's vehicle and Steve talking to the hospital on his radio.

"I'm sorry."

"No, no. You don't get to say that yet. We have a huge fight coming up and I don't want you to miss it."

She didn't respond, but he thought he'd seen a ghost of a smile cross her face.

"Come on. If you don't stay with me you automatically lose the argument and you don't want that now, do you?"

He wanted to touch her cheek, make her eyes open, but his only available hand was covered in her blood, the gauze pads completely soaked through.

"The hospital is ready for us. We're almost there." Steve turned in his seat. "How's she doing back there?"

"She's too damn quiet."

His own head throbbed and he closed his eyes, taking a deep breath, pulling on any final reserves of strength he had left. He looked back down at her. The color of her skin had turned ashy and the blood flow had slowed, from the pressure he put on her side or for a worse reason, he didn't know. His heart squeezed in his chest. What if...?

"Dammit, Cassidy, I'm not done talking to you, do you hear me? You've got to fight. You can't just bleed all over Jack's truck and call it a day. I didn't think you were a quitter."

The tires squealed as Jack pulled up and stopped at the ER doors. Hospital staff, waiting outside, rolled a stretcher right up to the truck. Steve climbed into the back seat and had to peel Bobby's cold, stiff fingers from her side.

"I've got her. I'll stay with her."

Bobby nodded as he watched them lower her from the truck and whisk her away.

Jack opened Bobby's door, helping him down, and walked with him into the ER. A man in a white coat steered them into an empty curtained area.

"Bobby, I'm Dr. Brooks."

"Yes, we've met before."

A nurse walked up to the doctor with a chart and handed it to him. "Thank you, Nurse Kelly and let's close this curtain. So, Bobby, Kate is not working today. Do you want me to call her in?"

"Absolutely not."

"Then let's get you on the bed so we can check you over." Jack and the nurse helped him to sit. Exhaustion and worry swamped Bobby all at once and he tilted too far, practically tipping off the mattress.

"Whoa." Jack held onto his shoulder. "You okay?"

"Just a little tired, Chief."

Dr. Brooks jotted notes on the chart. "Bobby, tell me about your injuries."

"My hand might be messed up a bit."

"Okay and what happened to your face?"

"Oh, Cassidy said after this happened..." he gestured to his damaged hand, "...that I hit my face on a table and my head hit the floor."

"Cassidy said? Does that mean you were unconscious when that happened?"

"I passed out, yeah."

Nurse Kelly, who'd been preparing supplies on a cart, rolled it closer to the bed. She took out a large set of shears and cut off the flannel shirt that Cassidy had used for a sling. Bobby saw a few stars when she pulled the fabric away from the dried blood, exposing his smashed hand.

"Shit. Did Drake do that? Himself?"

Jacks' voice had never sounded colder to Bobby.

"He did. With a brick."

"Let's take a look." The doctor slipped on a pair of gloves to poke at his hand.

Meanwhile, the nurse continued cutting until she could remove his now shredded uniform shirt. "Dr. Brooks, he has contusions all over his side."

"He'll need x-rays from just about his waist up and a CT scan. Please order those and I'll call the surgical department. They're going to have to bring in a specialist for that hand. Sit tight, Gentlemen."

"Hey, Doc? What about Cassidy?"

"I'll see if I can get an update for you." The nurse followed the doctor out, closing the curtain behind her.

Jack stepped closer to the bed. "What happened to your ribs?"

"August Drake sent me a fruit basket in jail. Those two guys that were arrested from the Brewhouse."

Jack nodded. "This is where I catch you up. Those two men and a deputy were found dead in a jail cell a few hours ago."

"What deputy?"

"I'm sorry, Bobby. It was John."

"Shit. John's the one who came to save me when those two cult members were using me as a piñata. He deserved better than that." Bobby shook his head at the loss of another good man. "It must have been the other deputy that brought them in cleaning up loose ends. Said his name was Baker. He definitely works for Drake. His nightstick left these bruises."

"You'll have to get me a description of this guy cause he's real good. He managed to turn off all surveillance cameras in the detention area, murder three men, and leave without alerting anyone."

"That asshole. He could be the one who killed Theresa, too." Bobby explained his theory about how his knife ended up in the killer's hands.

"That makes a lot of sense. Being as unstable as she was, she might have inadvertently caused her own demise. How many men did you say were at the drug house?"

"Drake, the driver, William, and two. Plus the two that brought Cassidy from the compound."

The nurse came back through the curtain with a wheelchair. "Can you give us one more minute, Kelly?"

"Sure, Chief."

Jack waited until she left again. "Was Cassidy there - voluntarily?"

"No. They brought her in cuffed with a bag over her head." Bobby could feel Jack's stare down to his bones.

"You know she's Drake's daughter."

Bobby had mixed emotions hearing that from Jack. Once again, his boss already knew information that he'd just learned the hard way, and yet, now Jack knew the whole truth and Bobby didn't have to withhold that information from him anymore.

"I found out a few hours ago. How did you find out?"

"I had a hunch and ran her prints. Then I went to talk to her at the Brewhouse. I wanted to get some background info on Drake and the cult. I told her we were going to shut down everything Drake was doing. That must be why she went to the compound."

"You think she went to warn them?"

"I'm betting she thought she could stop him."

Bobby rolled his neck on his shoulders. "How in the hell does she not tell me about him?"

"She didn't tell anyone."

"But, I'm..."

"You're what? A friend? With benefits? A temporary distraction?"

Bobby had no idea why he would find those words so offensive, but he did. "Is that what she said?"

"No. She said she figured you were going to punch out soon."

"What? Why?"

Jack crossed his arms. "Do I really need to answer that?"

"No, but... I don't think I'm ready to let her go yet. But, now she's ...."

"Don't give up on her."

Jack's phone buzzed. He read the screen, then cursed. "It's a text from Sean. Drake and his men are gone and they set the house on fire. Nothing turned up from the area search."

Doctor Brooks slid the curtain back. "Okay, Bobby, time to take you for x-rays."

"Any word on Cassidy?"

"She's in surgery now. We won't know anything for hours. Now, let's get you taken care of." He looked pointedly at Jack. "Everything else will have to wait."

CHAPTER NINETEEN

The dark, quiet hospital room was a welcome change from the last few days of doctors, nurses, needles, and surgeries. Bobby hurt everywhere, his hand the most. The fact that he might never regain full use of his dominant hand kept trying to settle in his brain so he kept pushing it further to the back. He couldn't think about that yet. On top of that, his ribs ached, his face hurt, and he had a headache that wouldn't quit, but he'd been told he'd live.

His mind kept spinning back to Cassidy. The possibility of her bleeding out on his lap had been legitimate. The thought of losing her, when he'd just found her, scared him more than anything. Part of him experienced vindication by his choice to always avoid relationships in the past. They were just too painful.

He couldn't deny that he missed her. A lot. He should be mad as hell at her, yet he just wanted to talk to her. He'd heard her surgery went well, but nothing more. He'd tried to leave his room twice to go find her and twice the nurses had tucked him back into his hospital bed. They were tougher than they looked.

The door opened and he braced himself for more nurse poking. Instead, his cousin, Kate, walked in with two tall cups of coffee. She put one on his table and rolled it closer to his left hand, pulling off the lid. Walking over to the window, she opened the vertical blinds half way to let in some light. Then she sat by his feet with her cup, stretching her own legs out next to his.

"Good morning."

"Morning. Thanks for the coffee."

"Sure. How're you feeling?"

He settled back against his pillows with his cup in hand. The smell of the strong coffee alone brightened his outlook. "Fine, Doc. How are you?"

"Well, I'm not lying to myself, like some people are, that's for sure."

"So says you."

"Are you in pain?"

He took a long sip of his coffee, and then another, just to keep her waiting. "No."

"Did you talk to your doctor?"

"Yes."

"And?"

Maguire women. Never happy unless they knew all the answers. One of the things he liked most about Cassidy, she didn't ask so many questions.

"Why do you ask when you already know?"

"It's like a quiz, to see if you were paying attention."

"Yes, I was paying attention when the doctor told me I have a mild concussion, and I need to take it easy until that heals. And, that my ribs are bruised not broken."

"True! Good answer. And?"

"And, I was paying attention when the doctor said my hand is fucked up, but not as bad as I'm sure Drake had hoped when he smashed it with a brick."

"Also true! Your x-rays show that several bones are broken, but it's the tissue damage that's severe."

"The doctor called it hamburger."

"Good description. My theory? Drake picked an old brick that had already begun disintegrating. Each hit did as much damage to the brick material as it did to your hand, making his weapon ineffectual. However, it did demolish the skin and tissue, almost tenderized it. In a way that's good, because it kept the bones from being pulverized beneath."

"That's disgusting."

"The body is an amazing machine and will heal a lot of that damage. For the rest, you now have stitches, pins, and screws holding everything together in there."

He looked at his damaged hand, elevated on a pillow. It only had a light dressing of gauze around it to keep it clean otherwise it resembled a swollen pin cushion and Frankenstein's monster all in one.

"He did say I'll never make it through a metal detector without it going off again."

"With some time, and the right amount of physical therapy, I think you'll be surprised at what you can accomplish."

He knew Kate wouldn't blow sunshine up his ass, so if she said his hand would get better, it would. That gave him some comfort. The door opened again and Maggie walked in with two cups of coffee.

"Now it's a party." Kate said, sliding off the end of the bed.

"Sorry, Kate, I should have thought to bring you a cup."

"That's okay, I just finished one and I'm late for work as it is. I'll just tag out and see you crazy kids later."

"Hell no, Doc. You tell my sister I'm fine before she asks me all the same questions that you did. She'll never believe me."

Kate looked from Maggie to Bobby and back. "He'll live."

Maggie smiled. "Well, that's the best news I've heard today."

"Right? I'll bring you some lunch later, Bobby. Lots of green gelatin."

"I can't wait."

Kate waved to them on her way out the door. Maggie set down a cup in front of him, then fished in her jacket pocket and pulled out a mobile phone.

"I charged it for you. We found your phone, wallet, and your keys in what remained of your clothes after your time in the ER."

Bobby stared at the phone she'd placed on the table. At the moment, using it with his left hand just seemed like too much of an effort.

Maggie sat in a nearby chair. "You'll live, huh?"

"That's what the doctors tell me. Any news on Drake?"

"If there is, Jack's being tight-lipped about it. You know him."

She took a sip of her coffee, watching him over the lid. He knew exactly what was coming next. Maguire women. Never happy unless they knew all the answers.

"Speaking of tight-lipped..."

"Were we?"

She smirked at him. "When were you going to tell me about Cassidy?"

He drank some more of his coffee. "What about her?"

"Don't be daft. About her parentage."

"Not my information to share."

"Ahh. Sweet. Even though you're upset with her, you still protect her secrets. So, it's true? Cassidy is Drake's daughter?"

"I can neither confirm, nor deny..."

"Yeah, yeah, yeah. I'm impressed though, that she was able to keep that secret all these years."

"Even from me."

"Which is also interesting, that you would care she withheld said information. Meanwhile, bachelor #1 *never* wants to know the histories of the girls he dates."

Truer words had never been spoken. Most of the girls he'd dated he already knew from town, but even if he just met them, he didn't want to know them beyond the few days they'd spend together.

"This was different. Drake's a criminal. He set me up for murder."

"Do you think she knew he would do that?"

Bobby shifted on the mattress. "Maybe. Maybe not."

"Did you ask her?"

"When should I have done that? While we were running for our lives or when she almost bled out in my arms?"

He couldn't hide that he'd choked-up on those words. He rubbed the fingers on his left hand together as he recalled how her blood had coated them.

"She's resting comfortably now."

"You saw her?"

Hungry for information about Cassidy, he sat up straighter in the bed. How times had changed for him. He'd been kidding himself that he could ever walk away from her. He'd been good and truly hooked.

"Yes, I did. I know she lost her mother recently and figured she might not have anyone else to stop in and check on her."

"She's really okay?"

"Yes, Kate says that physically she will fully recover."

"Is there a 'but' in that sentence?"

"I say this with all the love and respect I have for you as your sister. You screwed up big time."

Bobby shook his head. "Me?"

"You. As in, you need to figure out what you want before you break her heart anymore."

"What the hell are you talking about?"

"Here's what I gathered from my brief conversation with Cassidy and from knowing you my entire life."

Bobby made sure his sister could see him roll his eyes. "This should be stunning."

"Wait, wait. I think you'll be impressed. You see, Cassidy is a smart girl. She's heard it all and knows all about you. She probably expected the usual 'Bobby Maguire Whirlwind Relationship' package. However, this time you didn't play by your own rules. You stuck around. Gave her a glimpse of something new, something more. Until you find out she didn't fully disclose her entire life story to you. Which, by the way, you would never do. So, now you're going to ditch her and take that tiny bit of hope for the future with you."

He wanted to argue with her. He wanted to tell her how wrong she had the whole situation. In order to do that, he'd have to believe the opposite. He'd have to believe that he could have a real relationship with Cassidy.

"Well, when you put it like that you make me sound like quite the asshole."

"You asked."

"Not really. I'm amazed how you turned this all around and now I'm the bad guy."

"You don't have to be. Like I said, just take a little time to think about what you want before you do anything." Maggie looked at her phone and stood. "I need to get to a meeting. The election is just days away and people are starting to come out of the woodwork with crazy requests, proposals, and schemes. Why did I ever think going into politics was a good idea?"

"Don't stress. You got this mayor thing in the bag."

She stopped near the door to look back at him. "You do realize that this makes Cassidy and Rhys half brother and sister?"

"Not until just now." Cassidy would tell him his chances to pass the detective's exam were dwindling fast.

"It will be nice for them to have each other. Since she might not have anyone else."

She left before he could respond to her painful dig. It must be painful for a reason, right? Maggie's 'think before you decide' plan had merit, but it wouldn't work for him. He needed to talk to Cassidy. He needed to know everything, and he needed her to tell him.

CASSIDY LAY ON HER undamaged side watching the people walk past her hospital room door. It had to be the fourth, or maybe the fifth night, she'd been stuck in this room. The healing to her damaged side had been slow going thanks to an infection. The doctors told her it wouldn't be much longer and then have some gross discussion with her about her gunshot wound draining and antibiotics and when they would finally stich up the hole in her body. She couldn't be more thankful to the staff for saving her life, and taking such good care of her, but she wanted to leave so badly she'd started contemplating sneaking out during the nurse's shift change.

For not having many friends in Maguire's Corner, she'd had quite the 'A' list of visitors, starting with the O'Hart twins. They'd arrived at her hospital room with half the bar patrons in tow. Luckily, the nurses hadn't allowed them all in. Taylor and Tyler must have charmed their way into visiting with her and it took Cassidy pretending to fall asleep to finally get them to go home.

Jack had come alone to take her official statement starting at the moment she'd arrived at the compound straight through to the moment she'd been taken to the hospital. That had been the longest conversation of her life. More like an inquisition with him asking three questions to her every one answer. And, by the end, she couldn't tell if he believed a word she'd said.

Without having any difficulty with the 'family only' rules, Kate, Maggie, and Steve had all stopped by at different times to check on her. She hadn't had the nerve to ask them about Bobby and none of them mentioned his name. She missed him and she really wanted to see him. But, she would never forget the look on his face when he understood that Drake was her father and that she hadn't been the one to tell him.

A large man-shape blocked her view of the hallway. As if she'd conjured him just by thinking of him, Bobby stood in her doorway. Every fiber of her being awoke at the sight of him. Her heart burst open, joy flooding her inside. She couldn't deny how much he meant to her.

"May I come in?"

"Sure."

She attempted to sit up, but the tubes and IV prevented her from doing much besides scooting. She checked him all over, from his bruised face, to his bandaged hand in a sling, to the way he lowered his body into the chair next to the bed. She took him all in, happy to see him, yet, Bobby's blank stare gave nothing away.

"Are you okay, Bobby?"

"I will be."

"Your hand?"

"It'll heal."

The cold silence stretched between them like an old rubber band, threatening to snap at any moment. The stress might kill her.

"Are you okay, Cassidy? Last time I saw you…"

"You promised me an argument."

Bobby smiled. That helped loosen the ball of stress in the middle of her chest.

"I'll be okay."

"Good. Then maybe we should get right to it." He cleared his throat and straightened in his chair. "Why didn't you tell me Drake was your father?"

Even though she knew the question would be coming, it still surprised her, like she'd been sucker punched, pushing the air from her lungs. Mostly because this would probably be the last time Bobby would speak to her. Maybe this would be the best way for it to all end. Rip off the Band-Aid. It was kind of liberating. She'd just tell him the truth and it would all be over.

"I didn't want you to know."

"That's it?"

"Pretty much. The ol' 'Hi, I'm Cassidy and my weirdo dad leads a cult of weirdo followers in the woods' seems to put people off."

He cracked another smile. Small victory, but still a victory.

Bobby swept his hand to encompass himself. "I'm in a bathrobe. I don't have anywhere to go, so let's hear the whole story."

Cassidy sighed. "After my mom, Ruby, lost her fiancé to a drunk driver she had trouble ... coping. The charming and mysterious Drake found her in a bar drinking her life away. He listened to her and consoled her and convinced her to sell all her belongings and live with him in a rustic cabin in the woods. I was born a year later."

He shook his head. "You grew up there? At the compound?"

"Until I was about 13. We escaped in the middle of the night. Since we didn't have any money, mom pawned her only piece of real gold jewelry and got us a motel room. She found work as an off-the-books nanny. As soon as she could afford it she had my name legally changed to hers, Conklin, so no one would know who my father was. I started high school shortly after."

"Why wouldn't you tell me all this?"

"It's not that complicated. I didn't want you to know. I've never told anyone, because I don't want anyone to know. And, I figured, you wouldn't want to see me anymore once you found out."

"I'm not an asshole. Just because you're related to him doesn't mean I think you're like him. But, not telling me all this, it's huge. You knew what was going on. You knew I shot August, who I'm assuming is your brother. And you knew that Drake's minions were following me and reporting back."

Little bits of her happiness flaked away as Bobby's words grew angrier. "August is my half-brother. One of them."

"Did you know the two men that attacked us at the Brewhouse kitchen were from the compound?"

She had a strong need to move. She hated being stuck in this bed. "Drake has lots of new recruits up there. I don't know them all."

"That wasn't an answer."

"I didn't recognize them, but they told me their visit was a message from Drake."

Bobby slid to the front of his chair. "What? When? I took your police report. You never told me that you were threatened."

"Threatened? No, that was a Drake tantrum." She tried to roll to her back, but the throbbing in her side stopped her. This conversation hadn't gone the way she'd hoped. She couldn't worry how Bobby would react to her admissions, she just had to tell him the whole truth. Her heart had already begun to build shabby walls to keep from getting further crushed. "Drake, who I hadn't seen in years, who didn't even have the decency to come to my mother's funeral, shows up out of nowhere at the Brewhouse earlier that day. He wants me to come home, to move back to the compound. But, really, he doesn't. He just craves control, over everything. Property, people, especially his kids. He's nothing without that control."

While she spoke Bobby stood and moved to the end of her bed. He may have unintentionally put distance between them, but it broke her heart a little more.

"I told Drake to shove it, that I would never move back. Then he went on a little tirade. He knew Theresa had hurt me, he knew you shot August, and he knew I'd been seen with you. He told me I'd regret my words and he stomped off. When the two guys showed up later in the kitchen, one of them told me that Drake had sent his regards or something caveman-ish like that."

"I don't think you're taking this as seriously as you should, Cassidy. His 'tantrum' just put you and me in the hospital. He and his cult buddy, Baker, are now responsible for four murders in this town."

Her stomach grew queasy "I'm sorry. I didn't know."

"You realize he orchestrated all of this, right? He set me up so I would take the fall for Theresa's murder. They took my badge, Cassidy. They arrested me. Thanks to Jack I was released only to be taken straight to Drake at gunpoint for his 'eye for an eye' soliloquy."

Remembering how much Bobby had suffered, the torture that Drake had inflicted on him, brought tears to her eyes. "I'm so sorry.

I never thought...I didn't know what he would do. But, I did call the police."

"You what?"

"My whole life Drake has been saying stupid things. He rants and raves and blames everyone for his problems. It's just what he does and we all knew it was bullshit. This time was different, so I called 911 and told them that I'd overheard Drake make threats against the people of Maguire's Corner and that they should keep a closer eye on him."

"You left an anonymous tip? Jesus, Cassidy. You should have just told me."

"I should have." She wouldn't apologize again. She'd made her choices and now she'd live with them.

"Do you know what he's planning next? Because, this ain't over yet."

"No, I don't." She straightened the sheet, pulling it tight. "But, the way he was talking that day, I don't think his anger is aimed at just you anymore. I think he's mad at the whole town."

Bobby rubbed the back of his neck before his heavy gaze landed on her again. "Tell me what made your mother take her thirteen year old daughter out of the compound in the middle of the night."

He wanted the gory details, she would oblige. "Drake is addicted to these little pain pills and one day he tells me to go get the bottle from his truck. At thirteen I was more limbs than grace and I tripped, fell, and spilled the pills all over the gravel driveway. So, there I am, standing in front of this angry giant, my knees and hands cut-up and bleeding from my fall, and he's raging at me. I don't know if he expected me to cower, or to plead with him, but neither is in my nature."

She took a breath to steady herself noting that Bobby's good hand had balled into a fist.

"At the compound, men hurt women. Lots of verbal and physical abuse goes on. It's just the way it is. Drake would smack my mother just for looking at him sideways. So, I wasn't surprised that he hauled off and hit me, but once he started, it was like he'd had all this anger built up against me, and he just wouldn't stop. He beat me. Right there in front of half the compound. No one said a word or tried to stop him. When my mother found me she snapped and went after Drake with everything she had. His own guys had to pull her off of him. She swore that day he'd never lay a hand on either of us again."

"I'm sorry, Cassidy."

"It was a long time ago."

"But, it wasn't. He hit you at the house, didn't he?"

She could still feel the back of Drake's hand striking her across the face. It had filled her with shame, like she was a teenager again, but the shame quickly turned to anger. "I was hurling every insult and obscenity I could think of at him hoping he would stop torturing you and come at me. Then you passed out and hit the floor. I called him a thug and a coward. Apparently, that was one too many insults."

"Found him." A nurse hovered in the hospital doorway trying to catch her breath. "The police chief has had us searching the hospital for you, Mr. Maguire."

"Why? What's going on?"

The nurse moved and Jack walked up to Bobby, his frosty gaze taking in the whole room in an instant. "Drake busted August out of the county jail. We're putting the hospital on lock-down just in case they decide to come here for either you or Ms. Drake."

"Unbelievable. How the hell does he do that?"

"According to the guys at the Sheriff's department the Unite Today members drove their trucks right through the fences of the exercise yard, grabbed August out of his wheelchair, and took off, injuring two deputies in the process."

"Dammit!"

"All our officers currently on duty are on the way here."

"He won't come here."

Both men turned to look at her, their expressions inscrutable. Only cops could look through a person like they were doing now, as if you were a bug under a microscope.

Jack crossed his arms over his chest. "Why not?"

"He has no advantage here."

"You're assuming he's still thinking rationally, Ms. Drake."

"That's not her name."

Bobby had taken a step toward the chief and Jack smiled at him. "Yeah, I know."

Cassidy didn't know what to make of the two men squaring off, so she continued her response to Jack. "I know he's not rational, but he does think strategically. The hospital won't get him what he wants."

Jack nodded to Bobby. "What's she talking about?"

"Cassidy thinks Drake's anger is now aimed at the whole town."

"He's also a planner. He doesn't do anything on impulse."

"Then we better figure out his next move. Bobby, let's head to the surveillance room where we can keep an eye on everything while we talk. Cassidy, there will be an officer on your door until we're sure it's safe."

Jack left, but Bobby stayed a moment longer. "Thank you for telling me the truth." He walked to the door, stopped, started again, then stopped and turned toward her. "Since it's clear that I don't know what I'm doing, that I don't know how to do relationships, I'm not surprised to find out that I'm doing it all wrong. So, I think its best if I just stop before I do any more damage."

When he left the room, Cassidy could swear he took a part of her with him. Hot tears rolled down her cheeks soaking her hospital gown. She'd been wrong. Her heart could be crushed further. Until there was virtually nothing left.

CHAPTER TWENTY

Bobby couldn't decide if his extremely high stress level had been caused by his worthless right hand or by his boss being a jerk. Once he'd been released from the hospital, Jack had officially put him on 'light duty' and wouldn't cut him any slack about coming back to work full time if he couldn't hold and fire his weapon.

Bobby needed weeks of physical therapy to get his damaged hand in any kind of shape to even hold his gun, let alone pull the trigger, and they wouldn't start that until the swelling went down from his last surgery. However, the thought of not working, of not having something to take his mind off of– stuff – made him crazy.

In a moment of frustration, Bobby told the chief he could still out-shoot half the guys in the station left handed. Jack told him to prove it. So, here he stood, in the police department's indoor range, about to load his weapon with his left hand, his right all but useless, wrapped up like a mummy and hanging in the sling.

Jack stood to his right, next to the range controls. "Should I set the target for ten yards?"

"Sure. No problem."

With only one hand available, Bobby had to improvise. Standing the full magazine on end on the counter, he lowered the gun onto it, snapping it into place. Then using the gun's rear sights he racked the slide on the edge of the counter to chamber a round.

"We could do this another day."

"I got this, Chief."

Switching his grip, the gun started to slip from his hand and he had to use his thigh against the table to keep it from falling.

"Just going to dig yourself in deeper, huh?"

He had no intention of letting Jack see him fail. "You got something better to do, no one is stopping you from doing it, Chief."

"Are you actually pissed at me or would this have something to do with a certain brewmaster?"

"You're the one questioning my aptitude." Bobby had to set the gun down again to put in his ear plugs. He knew better than to let emotions rule him, yet, thinking about Cassidy made his gut lock-up. He took a breath to calm himself. "Clear. Range is hot."

Bobby waited for Jack to don his safety equipment before he picked up his gun again and released the safety. He'd shot with his left hand before, so he knew he would be capable, but it had been a while and he didn't spend a lot of time practicing.

His first shot hit low left. He adjusted and fired again. The remainder of his rounds all hit the silhouette, just not in the core target area. With the slide locked open on his gun he dropped the empty magazine and placed both on the counter.

"Clear. Range is cold."

Bobby pulled out his ear plugs, stuffing them in his pants pocket. "Don't bother to say it. That's not good enough."

Using the controls, the chief moved the target closer so they could both see it. "It may still be better than half the department, but it's not up to your standards."

Bobby rubbed at his forehead with the heel of his hand. "This sucks."

"You're pushing too hard. You need to give it more time."

"Time? How much of that do we actually have? No matter how much brainstorming we do, we have no idea when or where Drake will strike again. We don't have a clue where he is. It's been almost two weeks since he broke August out of jail and we can't find any of them."

"You're not alone here, you know? We're in this together."

"You're on your own, Jack. I'm freakin' useless." Bobby couldn't stop the words from pouring out. "I got my badge back and for what?

I can't work. I can't shoot. You don't trust me. Everyone in this town is in danger, my family included, and I can't protect any of them."

"I don't trust you?"

There went those damn emotions again, making him say stuff out loud that he meant to keep to himself. He decided to lay it all out for Jack.

"The moment we turned over that body and found out it was Theresa, you began to suspect me. You didn't want me at the crime scene and you didn't want me handling evidence."

"You're right. I didn't, but I don't suspect you, you idiot. I was protecting you." Jack stepped forward, pointing at Bobby. "You know what your problem is? You only see two feet in front of you. Let me lay out the facts. We shut down a major drug operation in town. You shot the son of the suspected ringleader. He starts having you followed all over town. A woman is brutally murdered. A woman you happened to date. Suddenly, all the evidence points to you? That stinks like conspiracy. You're just too close to see it."

A heavy weight lifted off Bobby's chest and he could breathe again. His best friend had been protecting him. He should have known that, but he'd been too angry. "Why didn't you just say that?"

"I did. Apparently you thought I was bullshitting you."

"You benched me without an explanation."

Jack shrugged. "Frankly, you were better off looking clueless. And, I had my suspicions about Cassidy. She was a new variable and I didn't know how she might fit into the equation."

Cassidy. The small ache, which had formed in his chest when he left her at the hospital, kept growing. He had no idea if she would look at him, let alone speak to him, but dammit, he missed her more each day. What he wouldn't give to turn around and find her behind him so he could grab her up in his arms and kiss that sweet mouth.

"I still don't."

"Sure you do. You're being stubborn and won't admit it. Stop acting like you're so damn innocent when you lied to me, and your family, about having a stalker. And, don't bother telling me it's not the same thing. You were protecting yourself and so was she."

"Geez, Jack, tell me how you really feel."

"I just did. You're my brother. I trust you with my life." Jack slapped him on the shoulder, walking toward the stairs. "Screw your head on right and focus on what's important. I'm going back to work."

Bobby waited for Jack to climb the stairs before he let out a huge breath and leaned on the wall. He'd worried about his relationship with his boss more than he'd wanted to, but Jack managed to alleviate most of his concerns within a few minutes.

They worked so closely, and so well together, he didn't want them to question each other's motives. Trust between them was paramount and Bobby would have to do more on his end to make sure Jack never doubted his level of commitment again.

And then, there was Cassidy. After hearing her side of the story, he understood her choices hadn't been easy. He hadn't made things any easier for her. Jack told him to quit being stubborn. Maggie told him to put up or shut up.

Bobby cracked his neck on each side. This would be the time he'd usually walk away. Relationships were messy and complicated. But, he couldn't do it this time. She'd gotten under his skin, and burrowed deep. No doubt about it, Cassidy held his misshapen heart in her hands and that scared the crap out of him.

THE HOT CUP OF COFFEE tasted so good Cassidy couldn't resist taking sip after gulp, enjoying the warming sensation in her chest, feeling the caffeine-induced brew burst through her body to her fingertips and toes, until she emptied the entire mug.

Even though the restaurant was having a busy Sunday morning, she didn't have to wait long before a waiter came by to give her a refill. The second cup she savored as she grew more excited about the huge lumberjack-style breakfast she'd ordered. She'd been home for days, but hadn't eaten more than cereal or soup. She'd been craving carbs, salt, and sugar since getting released from the hospital.

The new Dana's Family's Restaurant was small, but this building would be the temporary home of Dana's until they could rebuild on the blackened bones of the original structure. Cassidy had eaten at the first one plenty of times before it burned down. Poor Kate. She couldn't imagine being trapped inside a burning building and having to jump out a window to save her own life.

They'd seated her toward the back of the restaurant and Cassidy looked around to pass the time, her gaze pausing to enjoy a sketch of a maple tree in all four seasons hanging on the wall. It had to be one of Bobby's. A warm, happy feeling filled her when she thought of him, a huge improvement over the hopelessness she'd experienced when she'd told him all her secrets while lying in her hospital bed.

As if on cue, Bobby walked through the door of the restaurant and picked her out right away in the small space. He headed in her direction stopping every few steps to talk to his neighbors. Lots of gestures were made toward his hand which was still heavily wrapped, but no longer hanging in a sling. Although he looked impressive when he wore his police uniform, jeans, work boots and a button down flannel also made for some drool-worthy staring.

"Hi." She motioned for him to join her, pushing the chair across from her out a bit with her foot.

Bobby did a visual sweep of the whole room before he sat. "Have you been waiting long?"

"No, not too long. I'm only on my second cup. They're so busy I went ahead and ordered breakfast for both of us."

His eyebrows drew together which made that cute little 'v' appear over his nose. "Really? What am I having?"

"I told the waiter two orders of the 'BSB', the Bobby Sunday Breakfast. I remember you mentioning it when you were gloating about how many pancakes you can eat."

"My record still stands. They need to start a wall of fame and put my picture on it."

"That's a great idea. Maybe your Aunt will add the 'BSB' to the regular menu."

"It's definitely a 'Today's special' worthy item."

The waiter came over to the table with a fresh cup of coffee and placed it in front of Bobby. "Your breakfast is coming right up."

"Thank you." Cassidy nodded to him as he moved to the next table.

"How are you feeling, Cassidy? Are you all healed up?"

"Mostly. There's was some muscle damage so it will just take some time. Kate suggested that yoga might help strengthen my core. Down the road. How is your recovery going?"

"Slow." Bobby pointed to the white envelope on his placemat. "What's this?"

"I don't like to leave loose ends."

"That doesn't sound ominous at all."

"Relax. It's just payment for services rendered. I was able to catch up on a little accounting yesterday at the Brewhouse." Cassidy poured some milk and sugar in his coffee and stirred. "The envelope contains your check for the labels you created. It also contains a proposal for that mural I want you to do. You can peruse it at your leisure."

Bobby's frown had returned as he stared down at his mug. "You just doctored my coffee exactly how I like it."

"I should have asked first. I just figured you might need help." She sipped her own coffee trying to read his eyebrows. She couldn't tell if he was upset or just perplexed. "I like this new look. The scruff."

"It's hard to shave with this." He raised his bandaged hand. "It's hard to do anything with this. I'm not sure drawing murals, or drawing anything, will be in my future."

"The beauty of the future is that it's not here yet. We have no idea what you will accomplish."

"You sound like a fortune cookie."

As he sipped his coffee, Cassidy tried to decide which of the thousand questions she had, she'd ask first. "I bet you're missing the pool."

"Actually, my sister found this waterproof bag that makes an air tight seal around my arm so I went for a swim this morning. It felt great to get back in the pool."

"That's cool. I saw Maggie this morning."

"Last minute election party details?"

"She wanted to make sure everything was still on schedule, you know, after everything that's happened. She's really quite nervous about the whole thing."

"She shouldn't be. She's going to beat our uncle by a landslide."

"Cousin."

"Whatever."

Two waiters walked over, setting down two large plates of food in front of them and then a few smaller plates, mostly filled with bacon, anywhere they would fit on the table. "I'll be back with more coffee. Enjoy your meal."

Cassidy had to laugh as Bobby shook his head. "I may have ordered too much. I was so hungry when I got here and the smell of bacon was overwhelming. Please, help yourself."

Bobby's Aunt Dana walked over with a pot of coffee and topped off their cups. "How's my favorite nephew doing today?"

Bobby pointed to his plate. "He's wondering why his pancakes are already cut into bite-size squares?"

"I buttered and cut those myself, young man. I didn't want you to struggle with your breakfast." Bobby frowned up at her. "But, you can add your own syrup!" She patted him on the shoulder. "Good morning, Cassidy. You're looking well."

"Thank you, Mrs. Maguire."

"You know better than that. Call me, Aunt Dana. Now, eat up before it gets cold."

Bacon and pancakes were consumed in silence. Cassidy savored the delicious food. Having her recent brush with death, and worse, the terrible hospital food, made her appreciate it that much more.

"Watching you eat bacon is sexier than it should be."

She held a piece up. "There is no food in the universe more delicious or versatile than the slice of bacon."

"I missed that. Your humor." He smiled. "I miss you."

His smile warmed her. "I miss you, too."

Bobby finished his coffee and sat back in his chair. "I wasn't sure how you'd respond to my text to meet and talk."

"It was a surprise. I didn't expect to hear from you, let alone to share a meal." She straightened her cloth napkin across her lap while she gathered her courage. "I'm not sure where we went off track."

"I think we had some serious miscommunication. It's taken some time for me to move my pride out of the way and look at the facts."

"What facts are those?"

"That we made huge assumptions about each other, and what we expected, instead of talking to each other."

Cassidy shook her head. "Yes, we did. And, honestly, we're both better than that."

He held her gaze and then nodded. "As you said, we're worth more than a quick roll in the hay."

"Exactly."

"Do you mind taking a walk? It's crowded."

"I wouldn't mind at all."

CHAPTER TWENTY-ONE

Bobby left enough cash on the table for the bill and a generous tip, then followed her outside. The sun shone brightly, but it didn't warm the air at all. Cassidy pulled her jacket up higher on her neck. They walked for a few minutes before she spoke.

"So, if today's meeting is about communication, then I'm happy to start. I'm not going to accept your final pronouncement you made in the hospital that you're the only asshole here." She stuffed her cold hands into her pockets. "I am sorry, Bobby. I never thought beyond the moment with you. I didn't expect us to be anything more than a quick fling."

"That's my fault. I never told you any different."

"There's no one actually to blame. I don't think either of us saw this coming."

"Not a chance." Bobby rubbed the back of his neck. "I feel like we should have a big, angry, blow out, just get it all out into the open, and then we could clear all this up."

"I'd rather not have an argument when we're doing so well with this talking thing."

"Yeah, well, this talking thing is hard for some of us."

"Because you're mad?" He brushed his arm against hers and she leaned into it. "Tell me. What are you mad about?"

"I'm mad about the way you make me feel."

"That I make you feel mad?"

"No. I mean like feelings. The way you make me have feelings for you."

He made her head spin. What the hell did that mean? "You're not making any sense."

"I don't do feelings, Cassidy. Or relationships. At least, I never have ... before you."

"And now?"

"Now..." He took a minute before he continued. "Because of you, and these feelings, I want more."

Her crushed and broken heart fluttered in her chest. "Like what?"

"I want you. All of you." He looked up, like he was summoning the words from the sky. "I want you in my world. I want to share my things with you. Like today. Like Sunday mornings."

She sucked in a breath. "Swimming and pancakes Sunday mornings?"

He stopped at the end of the block and turned to face her. "Exactly. Family get-togethers. Football games. The shooting range." He moved a little closer. "I want to share these things with you."

"Are you still recovering from your concussion?"

"I want to be a part of your things, too. Your life. Your passions. I want you to share them with me." He brushed the backs of his fingers down her cheek. "I don't want to be alone."

His words were starting to imprint on her heart, her very being. "You don't?"

"No. I don't. Not when I know I can be with you instead."

An explosion rocked them sideways and up against the nearby building. The blast shook the street lamps, signs, and shattered windows all around them. Bobby turned their bodies just as a wave of debris overtook them.

HE STEERED THEM BOTH back down the sidewalk, the way they'd come, until they were clear of the dust. His ears buzzed and grit made his eyes and nose itch. What the hell had just happened? Holding Cassidy close he looked back toward where they'd been standing.

Across the street, the once solid stone structure of the Village Hall now had a giant rubble-filled front entrance. A small fire flickered inside one of the blown-out windows. Debris still fell on the ground along with papers and other unidentified bits.

Cassidy held her injured side while she coughed. Bobby reached for his phone in his pants pocket.

"Are you okay, Cass?"

She nodded to him, still coughing. He could feel the dust in his throat as well. He dialed dispatch at the police station.

"911, what's your emergency?"

"Jeff, this is AC Maguire. There's been an explosion at the Village Hall. Unknown cause. Unknown injured. Dispatch fire and ambulance. Notify Chief Munro."

Thankfully he didn't sound shaken up, but damn, if they'd been standing any closer? If they'd been on the opposite side of the street? Who knows what might have happened.

"Received. Village Hall. Fire. Ambulance. Chief Munro. Bobby, are you alright?"

"I'm good." A second detonation sounded, further away, yet Bobby still felt the ground shake beneath his feet. "Holy shit! Jeff, that was another explosion. Maybe northwest of my location? You know what to do." He disconnected his call.

Cassidy leaned on a light post. He checked her up and down. "You're really okay?"

"Yes. Just trying to catch my breath. You?"

"Yeah."

She shook her head. "I can't believe it. I can't believe he did this. This has to be Drake, right?"

"I don't know." He continued to scan the street, looking for Drake or his members. "I need a closer look at the building to make sure no one was in there. Do you want to head back to the restaurant?"

"And leave you alone? What if something else explodes?"

People were starting to walk in their direction, pointing at the damaged building. A few held their mobile phones. "Good. I'd rather have another set of eyes watch my back while I'm over there, anyway. Keep your phone out and if anything happens dial 911."

She pulled her phone from her pocket and held it up for him to see. "I'm on it."

He jogged down the sidewalk. He checked all directions for people, backpacks, or boxes that said ACME on them, then he crossed the street. He couldn't get as close to the entrance as he wanted, due to big chunks of masonry still falling off the building, so he had to settle for shouting into the structure.

He didn't expect anyone would be in the building on a Sunday, but he hadn't anticipated it blowing up either. Bobby listened close for any kind of response. Crying, rubble shifting, yelling, banging. Nothing. He tried the same thing in multiple places, but he never heard anything. Just the crackling of fire and falling debris.

Sirens were getting louder. Bobby walked back toward Cassidy. A larger group of people had gathered around her on the sidewalk, all with frightened faces.

Cassidy pointed to a man behind her. "Bobby, this gentleman heard that there was an explosion at the fire house."

Fear tore through him. What if the guys were there? What if Steve... He pulled out his phone again, but before he could call his cousin a woman from the back of the group spoke up.

"I just got off the phone with my daughter. She said there was an explosion at the elementary school."

There were gasps and mumbling as the small crowd grew more agitated. Bobby knew he'd have to keep these people composed while he hoped for the best.

"Okay, let's stay calm." Bobby held his hand up. "Remember, it's Sunday and most of these places are closed and completely empty."

An MCPD car pulled up near them, parked, and Officer Nick Ward climbed out. "Is everyone okay?"

"Yes." Bobby stepped closer to the vehicle. "No one here was near the building when the explosion happened."

"What about inside the building?"

"I got as close as I could and called out, but I didn't hear a response. Hey, aren't you on desk duty?"

"I am, so Jack sent me to pick you up."

"Good." Bobby motioned for Cassidy to join him. "Nick this is Cassidy."

"From the Brewhouse, right? Great beer."

"Thanks."

Another patrol car pulled up and parked on the opposite side of the street, followed by a fire engine. Bobby couldn't help but think of Steve. "Have you heard about any injuries?"

"Nothing at the four sites we know about."

"Four?"

"We have reports of explosions at the elementary school, fire house, community center, and the Village Hall."

"Why? Why would he do that?" Cassidy shook her head. "And why would Drake choose those places?"

Nick looked around before he spoke quietly. "Drake? We know that for sure?"

"No, but it's a good bet." Bobby turned to Cassidy. "You don't think he's just trying to cause chaos?"

"Like I told you, he's a strategic thinker. The fact that he's actually blowing up buildings is crazy, and I wouldn't have thought he'd have the guts to do it, but since it's actually happening I'm positive he wouldn't choose random buildings. There has to be a reason he chose these places."

Bobby ran his hand over his short hair while he pondered out loud. "Drake knew these would probably be empty on the weekend, so thankfully he wasn't looking for casualties or loss of life. They're all public buildings. Government buildings. Town buildings." His thoughts finally all clicked together. "Nick, Cassidy, let's get in the car."

Bobby turned back to speak to his neighbors. "Everyone, listen. We need to get all of you off the street while these guys do their jobs. Please, let's all head to our homes. If you see something suspicious, call 911. Stay tuned to the town emergency alert system. Any new information will come from there."

It took a few minutes for them to finally turn and head back down the street, then Bobby climbed into the passenger seat of the patrol car and dialed Jack on his phone as Nick backed down the street.

"Munro."

He took a minute to catch Jack up on everything they knew so far before he shared his theory. "Drake's upset at the whole town. Especially government officials. He thinks we're all corrupt and dishonest. What better way to fuck with us then trying to sabotage the election? The places he's targeted are all town buildings. All voting locations. And, if I'm right, there could be three more targets. The senior center, the library, and the town hall itself."

"That's our first solid lead. Have Nick take you to the library, I'll have a team head to the senior center, and I'll take a team to the Town Hall. Proceed with caution. We don't know how they're setting these damn things off."

"Copy that, Chief. Keep in touch." Bobby stuffed his phone back in the pocket of his jacket. "Nick, head to the library. Cassidy, I'm afraid we don't have time to drop you off."

"I told you, I'm not leaving you."

He turned a bit in his seat to look at her. "Do you know which of Drake's men would be capable of building these devices?"

"It's got to be this new guy you mentioned. Baker? Drake never had access to explosives before."

Nick looked over at Bobby. "Why would she know that?"

Bobby faced the windshield. "Let's just say my girlfriend has the inside scoop on everything Unite Today and today, I'm thankful for it."

"Girlfriend? Jiminy Crickets!"

Just like that she made him laugh and knocked down his stress level a bit. He made himself a promise, when this whole crazy situation ended, he'd do right by her. Dating, flowers, dinner, group therapy. Whatever she wanted.

CHAPTER TWENTY-TWO

Nick slow rolled the cruiser up the street that led to the library parking lot. When Bobby saw all the mini-vans and family sedans he broke into a sweat.

"The library's open." Nick said. "There's kids in there!"

"I see that. Let's keep calm. Do a sweep of the whole lot."

"Copy that."

They checked each car for occupants or anything out of the ordinary as Nick drove slowly through the parking lot. As they got closer to the building Cassidy put her hand on his shoulder.

"Look, over there, by the delivery door."

Nick stopped the car. "The mail truck?"

"A little out of place on a Sunday. Nick, find a place to park on the other side of the building."

"Okay, but what are you thinking?"

"Do you have a secondary weapon?"

Nick parked in a corner spot away from the entrance. "Yes and a shotgun in the trunk."

"We need to take down whoever is in that truck, quickly and quietly."

"Just the two of us?"

Bobby looked over his shoulder. "I'm betting Cassidy can handle the shotgun, can't you, Cassidy?"

"Are you basing that assumption on the fact that I grew up surrounded by gun toting idiots and that they might have taught me how to fire them?"

"I am. Can you?"

"Without a doubt."

The three headed to the back of the car. Nick handed Bobby a small automatic weapon he'd had holstered on his ankle then he opened the trunk. Cassidy took out the shotgun, checked the safety, loaded it with the shells Nick handed her, pulled back on the action to rack it, and then propped it on her shoulder.

Bobby had the urge to fan himself. "In case I don't get a chance to tell you, because we all get exploded and die, that was hot as hell."

With a soft puff of air she blew her bangs off her forehead. "Eat bacon. Load firearms. Check."

Nick slowly lowered the trunk until it latched silently. "Knock it off you two."

"Sorry. Focus. The less we are seen the better. Let's do this."

They fast-walked around the building, trying to avoid as many windows as possible. Bobby paused at the corner so he could observe the mail truck.

"Someone's in the driver's seat, suspect is male, talking on the phone," he whispered over his shoulder.

"Who is it?"

"I can't tell."

"Should we try to take him while he's still in the truck? Maybe he won't make it go boom if he's sitting in it."

"I like your idea, Nick. On three, you and I head straight for the vehicle. You take driver's side, I'll take passenger."

"Copy that."

"Cassidy, stay toward the back a bit to cover us both."

"Ditto. The copy, I mean. I copied, too."

"I got it. On three, two, one."

As soundlessly as possible, the three of them headed toward the mail truck. Bobby's heart raced in his chest and his brain buzzed with questions. Was he putting them in too much danger? Would this guy see them and hit the detonate button? Was this just the regular mail person and they were making a big mistake? Just before they reached the vehicle, the driver got out and walked toward the back doors of his truck.

"Freeze! MCPD."

Both Nick and Cassidy aimed their weapons at the suspect. Rage bubbled up inside Bobby as he recognized Baker, the deputy sheriff from the county jail. The one that loved leading with his nightstick and had killed his friend, John.

"Let me see your hands!"

"Maguire! Nice to see you. Or, should I call you Lefty? Don't tell me you're still mad about that whole jail beating thing."

"Uncle Mason?"

Baker faced Cassidy, his hands holding a piece of electronic equipment with wires hanging in all directions. "Cassidy? What are you doing here?"

"Baker! Carefully put down that device."

"That's not his name, Bobby. This is Drake's older brother, Mason Drake. My uncle. He hasn't been back to Maguire's Corner in years. He's in the military."

Mason squeezed his eyes shut and his face scrunched up before angry words burst out of him. "Not anymore. Dishonorably discharged after 15 years of dedicated service. 15 years. Can you believe that?"

"They finally caught you stealing inventory?"

"It was surplus!" He took a deep breath. "They accused me of 'Conduct Unbecoming' and then they took everything from me."

Cassidy nodded. "You sound just like Drake. Always blaming your shitty decisions on other people."

"You're comparing me to Dalton?"

"Who the hell is Dalton?" Nick asked.

"Drake is Dalton. His full name is Dalton Drake." Bobby took a step closer. "So, because you're pissed off at the military you're going to blow up the library with innocent people in it?"

"Pissed off? I'm more than just pissed off. I'm fucking vengeful. And no one is innocent, Maguire, you should know that."

"You murdered Theresa Wallace."

"Your little stalker friend? She was off the rails."

"She was a nice girl who needed help and you slit her throat." Bobby took a steadying breath. "You killed two of your own cult members and your murdered my friend, John. He had a family."

"Acceptable losses."

Bobby would never get through to a guy like Mason and he didn't want to waste his time on anyone wired so wrong.

Cassidy took a step forward. "There are little kids in there, Mason. I don't care what Drake told you to do, you can't kill little kids."

"Told me to do? My brother is a complete waste of space." Mason slammed his fist down on the device he held. "All these years he was supposed to build an army and instead he filled the compound with losers hooked on drugs and the old and weak. If it weren't for me, he'd still be up there crapping in his pants."

"You're taking credit for all this chaos?"

"It's a revolution, Cassidy. One you're on the wrong side of." Mason turned back to the mail truck and reached inside.

Bobby took another step and raised his weapon. "Don't move, Mason."

"I have a bomb. You won't shoot me."

The blast from the shotgun caught Bobby by surprise, shredding the open back door of the mail truck inches from Mason who dodged to the right. In seconds Cassidy racked the gun and had it pressed against her uncle's spine.

"I will. Move again."

Nick holstered his weapon and switched places with Cassidy, handcuffing Mason. Bobby checked the safety on his gun and then shoved it into the back pocket of his jeans, waiting for his heart rate to return to normal. He moved closer to Cassidy, appreciating her calm manner, and the way she held the shotgun down and away from everyone.

"How did you know he wouldn't kill us all?"

"He hadn't even finished putting the device thingy together yet."

"Device thingy? You're sure about that?"

Cassidy nodded. "Pretty sure."

Bobby's phone buzzed and he checked for a text message.

"It's from Jack. There's a situation at the Town Hall."

Nick held Mason by his upper arm. "What do we do with this Drake?"

"We'll take him with us. Nick, you need to evacuate this building. Get these families out of here without letting them know why. Call dispatch and see if they've requested the bomb retrieval team from the county yet and if not, make that happen. Also, if anyone is left available, send them to the Town Hall. Jack likes back-up

"Copy that, AC Maguire."

"Thanks, Nick. When this is all over, beer is on me."

CASSIDY FOLLOWED BOBBY back to the patrol car. They shoved her muttering, fuming uncle into the back. She climbed into the driver's seat, Bobby sliding in next to her.

"It's like a spaceship in here. Switches and sirens and computers, oh my!"

"First time in a cop car?"

She turned the key in the ignition. "First time in the front seat."

"I can't wait to hear that story, but first, let's go see Jack."

Cassidy drove as fast as she thought was safe. The closer they got to the location, the angrier she got. All this destruction and fear because of her stupid family. She was so glad she didn't inherit their idiot-gene.

Bobby put his hand on her forearm. "You've become uncharacteristically quiet over there. You good?"

"Not really. I'm mad as hell. How about you?"

"I get that. I'm pretty mad, but thankful no one has been hurt."

Cassidy sighed. "This is all so stupid. He's just postponing an election. He's not changing anyone's mind with these attacks."

"Even disrupting something as routine as an election can cause a lot of stress and fear in people."

Laughter erupted from the back off the car. "It's a revolution!"

"Shut up!" Cassidy would have laughed when they shouted it together, if things weren't so serious. "I'm sorry this is happening."

"Don't apologize for him, for either of them. This is not on you."

"I get that, I just hate that I'm related."

Making the turn onto County Route 13, Cassidy slowed the car so they could view the Town Hall building. The parking lot contained a few vehicles including a large, military-style truck parked haphazardly on the front steps at the entrance to the building and a police truck off to the side.

Bobby pointed to the side of the road. "Park over there, we'll walk up to Jack's truck."

"You want me to go with you?"

"Absolutely. Shotgun in hand. We'll leave Mason locked up in the back."

They made their way up the drive and to the truck, but Jack wasn't inside, so they kept walking toward the entrance. As they climbed the steps, she made sure to check all around them. Stopping at the front doors, Bobby pulled his handgun from his pocket.

"You ready?"

Cassidy raised the shotgun and chambered a round. "Right behind you."

After her eyes adjusted to the dim light inside, she could see Jack standing near an open doorway down the hall. She trailed behind Bobby, checking behind them every few moments. Before they reached him, Bobby whispered to Jack.

"Chief."

Without turning around, Jack lowered his hand by his leg and made a motion for them to stop. Bobby and Cassidy put their backs to the wall where they stood.

"Let them go, Drake. You don't want to do this."

Jack's voice sounded strained to Cassidy and then Bobby looked over at her and she was pretty sure he mouthed the word, 'hostages'.

"I didn't want any of this."

"No one's been hurt yet today. You can put an end to this peacefully."

"I think we both know we're beyond that now."

Hearing the front door open, Cassidy swung her shotgun toward the sound. Drake's right-hand man, William, walked in, his handgun pointed directly at them. Mason Drake barreled in behind him carrying a large, black rifle. Just as Cassidy said Bobby's name, Mason raised the rifle muzzle to the ceiling and let off three or four shots which echoed in the empty hallway.

"Trick or treat! Look whose back in the mix." He aimed the rifle toward them. "Just when I thought my partying days were over, here comes William to set me free!"

Cassidy kept her weapon aimed at William, trusting him far less than she did her uncle. "If you wanted a window left open, you should have just said so."

"You better find a way to shut that mouth of yours, little girl."

Bobby took a step toward him. "You don't get to talk to her like that."

"You picked a brave one, Cassidy." Mason tried to stare down Bobby, then he laughed out loud. "None of this is going to matter in a few minutes. Dalton! Where are you?"

"Mason? What took you so long? We're in the community room."

William moved closer. "You three, drop your weapons."

"Not a chance."

"Bobby." Jack nodded his head. "Do what he says. Please." Then he leaned down, setting his own gun on the floor.

"What? Why?"

"Just do it."

She watched Bobby struggle with Jack's request for more than a few moments before he finally complied. Left without a choice, Cassidy did as well.

William kicked their guns away and motioned for them to precede him into the next room. At the front of the room two podiums had been set up in front of rows of chairs. Interim mayor, Thomas Maguire stood behind the left one, his hands cable tied together. August Drake hovered next to him while leaning heavily on a crutch, his knee heavily bandaged. Maggie Maguire stood at the podium on the right in the same fashion with Drake looming over her.

CHAPTER TWENTY-THREE

"Mags."

Bobby headed toward his sister until Jack's hand on his right arm, and Drake holding up a stun gun, stopped him cold.

"Keep your distance, Maguire."

"What the hell is this? Why is my sister here?" Maggie looked cool and composed on the outside, but Bobby knew her Maguire temper would be keeping her all kinds of mad on the inside.

"We wanted to have a little chat with the current administration."

"We're on a tight schedule. Let's move this thing along," Mason said, standing somewhere behind Bobby.

"William, take their phones and then stand by the front entrance to make sure we're not disturbed."

Bobby handed his phone over, though he contemplated getting the jump on William. He just couldn't risk it with only one good working hand and so many other weapons in the room. A feeling of hopelessness took hold. The people he cared about most were all in danger and he didn't know how to help them.

"Well done, Dalton. I was sure you were going to fuck this up, too."

"Shut the hell up, Mason. While you were off playing soldier, the rest of us had to stay behind and hold down the fort."

"Which you did a terrible job of, by the way, brother."

"Do you know how much it costs to keep the compound up and running? Thousands every month. Bringing in new members after they sold off their estates worked for a long time, but then we were finding more and more with empty checkbooks." Drake pointed at Jack. "We had a steady stream of income from all those insurance claims on those houses that burned down and then you had to ruin that for us. Even my son's little side-job gets thwarted by Maguire's Corners finest. You can't seem to stop meddling in my business. So, here I am, meddling in yours."

"This has to stop. You're insane!" Cassidy threw her hands in the air. "What were you thinking? You could have hurt so many people today. Mason was going to detonate a bomb at the library. A library full of children!"

"Sometimes it takes something horrific and tragic to shine a light on an injustice."

Fear for all of their safety overwhelmed Bobby. They didn't have the numbers, they didn't have any weapons, and who knew if and when back-up would be coming. Absolutely anything could set these unstable men off. He had to keep Drake rambling so there would be time to figure something out.

"The problem with your statement isn't that it's true, it's that you believe that bullshit."

"It would have been a bold statement for the revolution!" August smacked his palm down on the podium.

"Revolution?" Cassidy pointed her finger at August. "The only thing revolting here is you, you strung-out-junkie-half-wit-loser!"

"Traitor!" Spit flew out of August's mouth when he shouted at Cassidy.

"Shut up, both of you!" Drake swung his arm, just missing Maggie. "You need to stop underestimating me, Maguire. You, and your family, always have. We are done with your rules. Done with your family ruling over this town. Look at this!" Drake pointed to Thomas and Maggie. "One replaces the other, replaces another. Why?"

"No one is stopping you, or anyone else, from running for the office."

It was the first words Maggie had spoken since they'd entered the room. Bobby had tried making eye contact with her, but she kept her eyes on the podium. He'd never seen her so withdrawn. He had to wonder if Drake had already used the stun gun on her. If Jack figured that out, there would be hell to pay.

"Let's have a little mock debate then, shall we?"

"We don't have time for this." Mason had moved closer to where Bobby stood in the middle aisle between the rows of folding chairs. Bobby could see Mason's rifle leaning on his shoulder, pointing at the ceiling.

"Just one question. Ms. Maguire, what makes you think you would make a good leader of this town?"

Maggie looked up at him. "You really expect me to answer that while you hold me hostage and threaten me with bodily harm?"

"Yes, I do. Now answer me."

"Fine." She cleared her throat. "We don't force the good citizens of Maguire's Corner to live the way we want them to live. A good leader recognizes when safety and security comes first and when it needs to take a back seat to personal freedoms."

"Personal freedoms? Like not being allowed to own firearms? Like paying outrageous taxes? Like swallowing the crap that is taught in public school these days? Those freedoms? I'll pass."

"When you choose to live in a civilized society, these are the social contracts that we make, that we agree to abide by. You can't make change by force. If you want things to change you have to work within the law."

"Don't you lecture me!" Drake shoved the stun gun against Maggie's shoulder, sending thousands of volts of electricity through her.

"No!"

As Maggie slumped over the podium, Jack launched himself at the older man, catching him right in the midsection, sending them both crashing to the floor. Without time to consider any consequences, Bobby picked up one of the closet chairs and swung it around trying to hit Mason. He managed to dodge it, only to get hit in the side of the head with a chair swung by Cassidy. Mason fell to his knees, dropping his rifle to protect his head when Cassidy swung the chair in the other direction, hitting him again.

"Bobby! He's going to kill him!"

The warning came from Tommy who had moved over to shield Maggie with his body. Bobby picked up Mason's gun with his left hand and moved closer to the fray. Drake had blood running down from his eye and a busted lip, but he'd managed to jam the stun gun into Jack's neck and he continued to hold the trigger down even though Jack was no longer responding to the jolts.

Bobby raised the rifle. "Drop it."

Drake looked Bobby in the eye and smiled, but didn't stop. Breathe in, finger on the trigger, breathe out, pull the trigger. The bullets ripped through Drake's chest sending him backwards into the wall.

"Dad!"

August took a step, but Bobby swung the rifle in his direction. "You lay your ass down on that floor or I swear I'll take out your other knee."

A commotion behind him had Bobby turning around in time to see Mason, back on his feet, grab hold of the chair that Cassidy was swinging at him again. As they wrestled with the furniture, Bobby moved to get a better angle, but he had no clear shot.

"I'm gonna kill your dick boyfriend for what he just did, Cassidy, and then I'm gonna kill you!"

Cassidy let go of the chair suddenly, sending Mason off balance. When he hit the floor she moved closer, raising her leg, she kicked him with her black boot, catching Mason right under the chin, blood and saliva shooting out from his mouth.

Cassidy stood over him and dusted off her pants. "You shut up!"

"Cass, I'll cover him, can you check on Jack?"

She moved to the front of the room and dropped down to Jack's side, then looked at Bobby over her shoulder.

"He's not breathing."

She didn't waste a moment and started chest compressions. Bobby scanned the entire room, but he didn't see a phone to call for help. Dammit. He thought about sending Tommy out of the room to find a phone yet he couldn't risk it because William might still be out there. Dammit.

"His vest." Cassidy tore at the Velcro sides of Jack's bullet proof vest. "It's in my way. Come on, Jack."

Cassidy continued, but Bobby could already see her tiring. Gun shots and shouting sounded from outside. Footsteps were heading toward them. Bobby lifted the heavy rifle again, this time to aim at the doorway.

"MCPD. Lower your weapons. We're coming in."

"Rafferty?"

Sean came around the corner. "Bobby. Back-up has arrived. We're all clear out here."

"Take over for Cassidy. Quick."

Holstering his weapon, Sean headed right to the front of the room. More police officers followed through the door and Bobby handed off the rifle to one of them. Sean made Cassidy stop while he checked for a pulse.

"He's got a pulse. He's breathing."

The fist holding his own heart from beating finally released and Bobby took his first deep breath in what seemed like hours. Sean called on the radio for an ambulance while Bobby walked over to his sister. He put his arms around her as soon as he got close enough.

"You okay, Mags?"

"I think so. That hurts so bad. Jack needs to go to the hospital."

"You both do."

Nick walked through the doorway. "We need to evacuate this building right now. That truck out front, it's rigged to blow."

The laughter that erupted from Mason as he lay on the floor, now on his stomach, his hands cuffed behind his back, had to be the most evil sound Bobby had ever heard.

"How long?"

"Minutes."

Seconds ticked by as Bobby looked around the room, recognizing every important person in his life. He had to do something to help them. He had to protect them. With Maggie and Jack hurt, it would take longer than a few minutes to get them all to safety. It wouldn't take long to move the truck.

"Nick, where is William? Their lookout?"

"On the front steps. Deceased."

Bobby took another second to make eye contact with Cassidy before he ran out the room and down the hallway. Reaching the front doors he saw that officers were moving patrol cars away from the building. William's body lay face down on the steps. He quickly checked the dead man's pockets, each moment wondering if the truck would just explode and take them all at once.

His hunch paid off and he found the truck's keys. He ran to the driver's side and climbed in, then cursed as he realized the truck had a manual transmission and his shifting hand couldn't do the job. He'd have to make it work. Pushing the stick shift into first gear with his left hand, he jammed his foot down on the clutch pedal then started the truck.

Not knowing how much time might be left, Bobby drove the truck off the front steps of the Town Hall, passing the ambulance that had been stopped at the entrance, and on to the main road. Taking the next turn he drove the vehicle passed the recycling center, down the road to where the town kept the piles of sand for the icy roads in the winter. He braked hard, threw the truck in park, jumped out, and ran.

In a way, he was glad he couldn't see the timer. At this moment he knew he'd finally done everything in his power to keep those he loved safe. Cassidy included. The explosion didn't surprise him until the blast swept him off his feet, tossing him to the ground.

CHAPTER TWENTY-FOUR

The only thing keeping her body moving at this point had to be the adrenaline. Cassidy had never wanted to lie down and sleep so bad in her entire life. This day didn't seem to want to end. Pacing in the ER waiting room, patiently awaiting news on just about everyone, she considered how lucky they all were for making it this far.

"Cassidy." Kate Maguire called her over to the desk. "Here are your updates. Jack is doing well, but we're keeping him overnight to run some tests on his heart. Just to be sure. That stun gun was a homemade job meant to do more than just incapacitate. It could've killed him. Maggie is fine and will be released shortly."

"Finally, some good news. What about Bobby?"

"Didn't anyone tell you?"

Cassidy's lungs seized in her chest. "Tell me what?"

"He's never going to stop being a jerk-face. We can't help him here for that."

"Jerk-face?" She smiled and took a deep breath. "That's the best you can do?"

"Just trying to keep it PG in here. This is my workplace."

"Thank you, Kate."

"No, thank you, Cassidy. I know what you did for Jack."

"When we opened the Brewhouse , the twins and I took a first aid course and learned CPR. I never thought I'd actually have to use it."

"You may want to keep that certification current. Especially hanging around the guys."

"Jack and Bobby are like crazy heroic, and full of stupid, all at the same time."

"Perfectly stated. I will now have that printed on t-shirts for the holidays." Kate put her hand on Cassidy's shoulder. "I'm sorry about your father."

"That's sweet of you to say, but I'm not."

"Rhys said something similar when I told him. He'll be home this weekend."

"He will?" Cassidy took a deep breath. "Did you tell him? That we're related?"

"I did. I wanted to tell him what was going on before he heard about it from someone else."

"I get that."

"And, before you get weird about it, Rhys is going to love having you for a baby sister."

"Thanks." Cassidy shook her head. "Weirdest family reunion. Ever."

"Cass."

She spun on her heel to see Bobby standing a few feet away. Larger than life, her favorite police officer, with a few new scrapes and bruises from his face-plant on the road after the truck exploded. Otherwise, he looked amazing to her. Her heart swelled as she stepped into his arms, finally feeling at peace after the day they'd had.

"I'm so glad you're okay." She looked up at him. "Are you okay?"

"Yeah. My hand got a little banged up from the fall. Got a new dressing for it and a stern warning from my doctor. Everything else is superficial. Are you okay?"

"I'm fine. Just really tired."

"I could sleep for a week. There's a patrol car here to take us home. I'll worry about paperwork, and just about everything else, tomorrow. Maybe the next day."

"Home?"

"Mine or yours. I'm easy. But, we go together."

"Then yours. I don't have any food at mine. Or furniture for the matter."

Cassidy held tight to Bobby on the ride to his apartment. There'd been so many times during the day that they could've died at the hands of her family. She just needed reassurance that they were both still breathing. When Bobby opened his front door it looked like the place had been ransacked.

"Sorry for the mess. I had a little trouble keeping the place neat with just one hand."

"That can wait for tomorrow, too."

They took off layers of clothes, leaving Bobby in his boxers and Cassidy in a clean t-shirt. Snuggling down in the covers with Bobby actually brought a tear to her eye and she had to bite her lip to keep from bawling. He scooched a little closer, pushed and pulled her, until he had her on her side, facing him.

"I missed this, Cass. I missed you. A lot."

"It's my fault."

He shook his head. "It's not."

"It is and I'm sorry. For everything. For my family."

"Don't. You had nothing to do with them and you're nothing like them. I know that. I'm the one who's sorry, Cass." He nodded as she shook her head. "I had no choice but to shoot Drake. I feel terrible that you had to see it."

"I would have done it. I will never hold that against you."

"I believe that. I'm sorry for that, too." He brushed some of her hair off her cheek to behind her ear. "You were amazing today. I'll never forget the way you handled yourself. And handled that shotgun. You saved lives. You saved Jack. You had my back. Thank you."

"Yep. I was pretty bad ass today." His smile warmed her.

"Listen, I know I have no right to hold your omissions against you when I flat out lied about having a stalker. To everyone. That's all over. But, if there is anything, absolutely anything, left that we need to tell each other, I suggest we do it right now. No more holding back information."

Cassidy sighed. "I do have one more thing that I need to share with you."

"You do?"

"I do." She made sure to pause for effect. "And, it's big."

"It is?"

"It is." He looked confused and hurt, so she decided to put him out of his misery. "I refuse to be the kind of girl that's just another notch on Bobby Maguire's bedpost." She knocked on the wooden headboard of his bed with her knuckle.

"You refuse?"

"Unequivocally. However, I am the kind of girl who will ruin you for all other women. If you want me, you have to want all of me, the good parts and the bad."

"Thank the universe." He pulled her in closer. "I especially want your bad parts."

"No joke, Bobby. My heart is so full of love for you, I honestly can't contain it. If you're just going to set me aside when you get bored, save me the heartache."

"Bored?" He shook his head. "You could never bore me, that's why I love you, Cass."

She gasped. "Oh! I knew you were sweet on me."

"Aw, shucks, baby. You know I am."

Cassidy met him half way, his lips softly meeting hers for a kiss full of laughter and promises.

EPILOGUE

The Brewhouse hummed with excitement and anticipation as Bobby walked through the bar area to the private room his sister had rented. He skirted the crowd and headed to the mini-bar and ran right into Jack.

"Fancy meeting you here."

Jack handed him a beer. "It's about time you showed up."

"I've been a little busy trying to fill both our shoes." Bobby took a huge gulp of his beer. Ah, Cassidy beer. He'd never drink store bought again. "Did you get cleared by the doctor today?"

"I did. All my tests have come back normal or within acceptable parameters. In other words, my heart is fine. I'll be back to work tomorrow."

"Good. Then why do you look more nervous than a long-tailed cat in a room full of rocking chairs?"

"It's nothing."

"Is it the election, cause she pretty much has this in the bag."

"No. I've been calling her the mayor for months now. It's not that."

Bobby did another visual sweep of the room. Jack didn't normally avoid his questions. "Do you suspect something might happen tonight?"

"No. Stop digging. You're as bad as the girls."

"Ouch. That hurts. I thought we were brothers?"

"Fine." Jack looked around, then leaned in closer. "There's a small jewelry box burning a hole in my pocket."

"What the..." Bobby smacked a hand over his own mouth.

"You make a scene and I'll kill you."

"Okay, okay. When are you gonna ask her?"

"Later. Maybe. When we get home. I don't know. This is her big night. Maybe tomorrow. I don't want to wait much longer than that. After all we've been through I just need to do this. You know?"

Bobby truly understood. All too well. These last few years had been a constant reminder that life had a way of sneaking up and biting you on the ass. The last few days only proved you had to hold on tight to the people you loved. He held his bottle of beer up to Jack's. "I agree. It's about time. You did ask my mom, right?"

"Of course I did. You and me, we're good?"

"Better than good."

"Bobby! What took you so long?" Maggie's smile lit up the whole room as she walked toward them. Bobby leaned down so she could kiss his cheek.

"Sheesh. I got here as soon as I could."

"It's just getting late. You two looked so serious when I came over. We're you telling Jack about work?"

"Work? Yes, I was just telling Jack about how busy it's been. I'm pretty sure we've blown the overtime budget for the rest of the year. We've managed to round up the rest of the cult members and shut down their drug operation for good. The nice part for me is getting to dictate all my reports and someone else gets to type them in to the computer. On the other hand, there's been an uptick in calls about suspicious people and false alarms. People are still scared."

"Of course they are." Maggie smoothed her hands down her dress. "They can't drive anywhere in this town without seeing a building destroyed."

Jack took her hand in his. "Thankfully, it was only four buildings instead of seven."

"See, Mags, there's your silver lining. Those last three locations were able to accommodate all the voters in town for you to hold your little election."

"Do you think that's what people think, Bobby? That it's a 'Maguire' election? I mean, Drake said the same thing. Do you think we need to take a step back?"

"In a town that's named after our family? No." Bobby took a sip of his beer and a second to reign in his anger over Drake's words emanating from the grave. "You know, I don't hear a lot of complaints on a normal basis about what we do around here. We may own lots of businesses and hold lots of important positions, but we also work really hard and volunteer lots of our time. We only want what's best for this town."

"You're right, I know."

"Of course I'm right. Can we please not discuss Drake anymore? Especially tonight."

"I'm good never hearing the name again," Jack said.

"I wasn't trying to bring the party down. Just trying to be proactive. This is a huge responsibility and it needs to be done right."

Bobby tipped his beer toward her. "Dad would be proud of you, Maggie. When you question your motives, or your will, think about him."

Emily came over and touched Maggie on the shoulder. "Your poll watcher just came back with some last minute numbers. I'll put them on the whiteboard."

"I'll come with you. Excuse me, gentlemen."

"Gentlemen?" Jack shook his head. "It's like she doesn't know us at all."

Bobby finished his beer. "I'm going to find Cassidy. I'll see you back here shortly."

Getting back through the room took longer than he thought as his family members kept stopping him to talk. Most of the conversations were the same. How was his hand? What happened to the Drakes? What about Unite Today? When would they start fixing buildings? Was it true he had an actual girlfriend?

Listening to Steve with half an ear, Bobby looked up to see Cassidy walk in with a case of beer and head to the mini-bar.

"Steve. Cut to the chase, will you. My girl's over there and I need to be where she is."

"That's just fuckin' adorable. My point is the guys and I can patch up the damage to the firehouse, until the time comes to actually fix it, but we need to relocate at least one piece of apparatus."

"If you want permission to move stuff to any of the town buildings, you're talking to the wrong sibling."

"I don't need you to talk to Maggie, I've got her wrapped around my finger. I need you to talk to Jack about using the police garage. It's a better location and it's got security."

"Oh, okay. I will bring it up with him tomorrow."

"Thanks, buddy."

Bobby shook his head as he walked away. When he decided to be a cop in a small town, he knew it wouldn't always be minute to minute excitement, car chases, and catching bad guys. And now that he'd had quite a few of those dangerous and exhilarating experiences, he wouldn't mind going back to those regular days with regular problems.

Disappointed he could no longer see Cassidy, Bobby left the room and headed to the main bar where he found her talking with the O'Hart twins. Taylor had his arm casually thrown around Cassidy's shoulder. Bobby waited for the jealousy to hit, yet it didn't come. It may have had something to do with the way she held his gaze, like there was no one else in the room but him.

Tyler put out his hand to shake Bobby's, but Bobby held up his bandaged hand. "Sorry about that. It's getting better?"

"It is. Thanks."

"We were just checking with Cassidy on how things were going at our first private event."

"The room looks great. You guys did an amazing job in a short amount of time. I think Maggie is really pleased."

"That's good to hear." Taylor gave Cassidy a quick squeeze and then released her. "Hey, we don't know who to talk to about this, but keep us in mind for any of the upcoming construction in town. Things here at the Brewhouse are steady and we wouldn't mind the outside work."

"I'll pass that information along. Your expertise will be greatly appreciated."

Cassidy took the bar rag off her shoulder and spun it like she might snap it. "You boys can get back to work now. Those glasses at the bar aren't going to fill themselves."

Tyler pushed Taylor toward the end of the bar. "See you crazy kids later."

Taking his hand, Cassidy led Bobby down the hall. She snuck them past the election party to an empty room, and then pressed up against his chest, wrapping her arms around him. He held her close, just breathing her in.

"How was your day, Cass?"

"Long, but extremely gratifying. Yours?"

"Actually, the same. This right here is the best part." He squeezed her a little tighter. "You changed your hair."

"I did. Thanks for noticing."

"I dig the blue streaks."

"I had a feeling you might."

She looked up and he kissed her, his tongue nudging her soft lips open and slipping between them. He immediately wished they were somewhere much more private. They'd been too tired the other night to do any more than share a goodnight kiss. He wanted to rectify that, and soon, but he'd also made a promise that when everything calmed down, he would do right by her. He ended their kiss before he got too carried away.

"Still love me, Cass?"

"Marginally more than I did yesterday."

Jack's words about not wasting anymore time kept replaying in his head. "Move in with me."

She raised her eyebrow at him. "Are you sure that request isn't just a reaction to our recent crisis situation?"

"No, I'm not sure." He smiled down at her. "I want to make this relationship work and I don't think it makes much sense living apart when we want to be together. I love you and I want you with me."

Cassidy shrugged. "Okay."

"Good. I'll call for a moving truck."

"Don't bother. I don't own much. Mostly clothes and some personal items. Two trips with my car ought to do it."

"A low maintenance kind of girl. How did I get so lucky?"

He held her tight. More than lucky, Bobby was truly happy. He didn't want this moment to end.

"Someone is shouting your name down the hallway."

He continued to hold her. "I hear them."

"I think the election might be over."

"Mmm hmmm."

"I'll have to get the champagne out."

"Right. To celebrate the winner."

"Come on. This is your sister's big day."

Cassidy dragged him back to the other room. As they walked through the doorway a phone started to ring. Maggie stood near the center of the room, Jack by her side. She looked down at her mobile. "It's the Board of Elections calling." She touched a button then put the phone up to her ear. "Maggie Maguire." Silence filled the room as they all waited. Maggie looked up at Jack, a huge smile breaking across her face. "I did?"

The End

ABOUT THE AUTHOR

Heather M. Gardner's love of books began on the hand-woven rugs of her small town library where her mother worked. There she had a never-ending supply of stories to read at her fingertips. As a teen, her favorite genres to curl up with were romance and mysteries. When she started to create her own stories, they were the perfect fit.

Heather resides in New York with her best friend, who is also her husband, plus her talented and handsome son. She is currently owned by one bitey rescue dog and two crazy rescue cats. Heather's a chocolate enthusiast, coffee junkie, pet addict, book hoarder, and fluent in sarcasm.

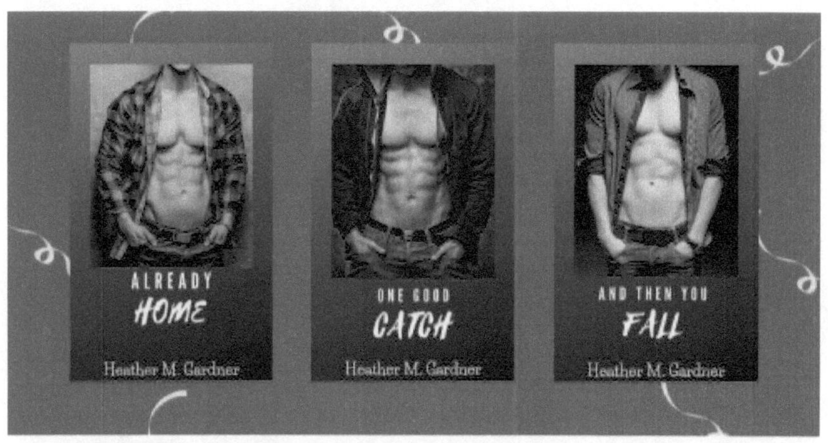

YOU CAN'T STOP AT JUST one! Read the entire Maguire's Corner series!

Already Home
One Good Catch
And Then You Fall